This Isn't About the Money

This Isn't About the Money

Sally Warner

SCHOLASTIC INC.
New York Toronto London Auckland Sydney
Mexico City New Delhi Hong Kong Buenos Aires

ISBN 0-439-67033-0

Text copyright © 2002 by Sally Warner. All rights reserved. Published by Scholastic Inc., 557 Broadway, New York, NY 10012, by arrangement with Viking Children's Books, a member of Penguin Group (USA) Inc. SCHOLASTIC and associated logos are trademarks and/or registered trademarks of Scholastic Inc.

12 11 10 9 8 7 6 5 4 3 2 1   4 5 6 7 8 9/0

Printed in the U.S.A.   40

First Scholastic printing, October 2004

Set in Excelsior
Book design by Nancy Brennan

This is a work of fiction. The characters and events in this story are not based on real people or events.

$\mathcal{A}$CKNOWLEDGMENTS

I thank Emily F. Davis, Esq., for her research into Arizona's laws and procedures and for her concise interpretation of that research. I also thank David Denenholz, M.D., for his generous help in outlining a typical course of treatment for the injuries described in this book.

Any legal or medical errors in the book are my own.

Finally, I thank Daniel Gaard for helping me when I was exploring Flagstaff, Arizona. His informal map and comments were very useful.

To the memory of Quetzalcoatl,
who died, and to Tonantzin,
who woke up in the desert—and lived

CONTENTS

CHAPTER ONE

Missing Moon

The sand was cold.

Strange, Janey thought. This was the desert, and desert sand should be hot. She scooped up a gritty handful and let it trickle through her fingers, which were also cold. It was such a dark night that she couldn't even see the grains of sand as they fell.

This was not like playground sand. This sand felt mean.

There were stars out, though, and they seemed to wink kindly at Janey. One great wash of starlight smeared across the black sky in a giant arc, and thousands of little stars surged toward it as if wanting to get in on the action.

No moon. Where was the moon?

Her head hurt. "My head hurts," she tried to say aloud, almost as an experiment, but the words could not make their way past her lips. And there was something even more important than the hurting, Janey thought suddenly, something she had to remember. She shook the last grains of sand from her hand and—as if it might help her memory—she touched her face.

Sticky.

Why, she wondered, was she sitting cross-legged on the cold sand in the desert in the middle of the night?

All alone?

What was it she'd forgotten?

And where was all the noise coming from?

"Oh, my god—that Toyota's completely flipped over. It went right through the barbed wire, and it's smashed flatter than a—did someone call 911?"

"I'm talking to 911 now! The lady says—"

"Shine your headlights over here. I can't see if there's anyone—"

"Don't you get too close to that car, Frank. What if it explodes?"

"Did you see that SUV swerve over the center line? Brand-new, too. What in the world—"

"I've got the driver right here. Not a scratch on her, but she's stinking drunk."

"Lemme go. I din do anything wrong. Let go my arm."

"Jeez, lady."

"I don't hear any sirens! What's taking them so long?"

"What do you expect? We're in the middle of the desert. Nearest town must be almost ten miles back, and I didn't even see a gas station there, much less a hospital."

"That was Aguila. It's barely even a town. They have a volunteer fire department, I think, but this looks too serious for them to handle. If anyone's still alive, they'll have to be airlifted to Phoenix. The 911 woman says we're supposed to see if anyone needs CPR."

"Don't you even think about it, Frank Benning—you get back up here right this very minute. I think I'm going to be sick! No one could be alive in that car, and there's no point you getting killed, too. I can smell the gas from here—it's gonna blow up, just like in the movies!"

"Stop yelling, lady. You're not making it any easier for him."

"Well, he's not your husband, is he? Why should I make things easy for him? We've got three kids at home!"

"*I've got kids, too. And there could be kids in that car, did you ever think of that?*"

"*I think there's two people in the front seats, but I can't tell for sure. If they're in there, they're not moving. And the back of the car is so smashed up that I can't make out if—can we get more light over here?*"

"*I tol you, let go my arm! It wun my fault. I'm a good driver, ask anyone. Why does everything have to happen to me?*"

"*You're a lousy driver, and you're drunk as a skunk. If you wasn't a lady, I'd pop you one.*"

"*Don' you threaten me. I'll tell my husband on you, and he'll—*"

"*Lady, those people are probably dead! Don't you get it?*"

"*You can't talk to me like that! I'm goin' home.*"

"*You're not going anywhere.*"

"*Frank, I think I see—*"

"*Fire!*"

Snakes came out at night in the desert, Janey remembered. If she actually saw a snake, and if she lived to tell the tale, she could just casually mention it to everyone at school—well, in her class, at least—

and pretend that it had been no big deal. Ramona and Stacy would think that was pretty cool.

No, wait, Janey thought dully, school was over. It was July, and she and her family were on their way from Flagstaff, Arizona, to Glendale, California, to see Grandpa and Aunt Baby, Grandpa's younger sister. Poppy's aunt.

"Aunt Baby." Janey could almost see her mother's wry smile as she said the name. Aunt Baby and Norrie Bishop had never gotten along.

"But I don't want to go to California now," Janey had told her mom. "It's almost my birthday. I want to stay home and do something fun with my friends. Stacy's dad said he'd take us camping in Oak Creek Canyon."

"We'll celebrate your birthday at Disneyland this year," her mother promised. "Now don't fuss, Miss Jane—you know how your father feels about family, and he doesn't ask for a whole heck of a lot. He'd be so sad if you didn't come with us. And if I can make this blasted trip, you certainly can," she added under her breath.

Her parents decided to make the long drive at night. Well, you just about had to drive at night in Arizona when you were planning to go through the desert and it was as hot out as it had been. Over 110 degrees in Phoenix, four days in a row! Much cooler in Flagstaff, of course, but Grandpa and Aunt Baby didn't live in Flagstaff.

Which was probably a very good thing. Aunt Baby always complained that Flagstaff gave her a headache. Something about the altitude.

Janey nodded once in the dark, as if she had just finished adding up all those big temperature numbers in her head. "Ow," she whispered, surprised.

Although they'd left home after ten P.M., Janey remembered, it was still warm out—even in Flagstaff. That's why they'd rolled down all the car windows. Then she and YoYo had fallen asleep in the backseat, seat belts fastened. YoYo was wearing her nightgown, and she'd been clutching Mousey and trying valiantly not to suck her thumb.

YoYo.

Where *was* everyone?

Janey frowned a little, trying to think. Broken creosote bushes filled the air with their pungent odor, so much like the smell of burning brakes, and they mingled with—with something else. What was it? Gasoline?

She had to ask someone. "Mommy?" she said, but the word sounded more like "Murm?" as she uttered it.

Janey blinked at the sound she had made and slowly moved her head, searching for her mother. Her gaze settled briefly on an unimaginable scene some distance away, and she shook her head slightly, averting her eyes. "Hurts," she announced again, as if someone else were standing right there. The word came out very clearly this time.

She closed her eyes.

"Janey?" Soft as it was, her little sister's voice seemed to slice through the desert night.

"YoYo?" Janey said, opening her eyes in wonder.

In front of her, her sister's round white face glowed like the missing moon. Her sturdy body—clad only in a fluttering white nightgown—seemed planted on the desert floor, as if it belonged there.

Janey tried to smile. "YoYo," she said again, pleased with the success her mouth made of the word.

"What's the matter with your face?" YoYo asked. She sounded scared, and her eyes were open wide.

Janey touched her face once more. Still sticky. "I don't know," she said, puzzled.

"What?"

"I don't know," Janey said, louder.

"Stop saying 'No no' at me." YoYo backed up a step. "I want my Mommy. I want my Poppy."

"Don't be scared."

"Stop talking at me with your red mouth!"

YoYo's face was getting smaller by the second, Janey noticed. She wanted to reach out to her little sister, touch her cheek, maybe, but she couldn't remember how anymore.

She was very cold now, and people were shouting fire, fire.

Janey felt the blast from where she sat. The desert floor seemed to lift a little, then settle back into itself.

"Mommy!" YoYo was screaming when the roaring stopped. She stumbled toward what was left of the Toyota, arms out and fingers spread wide, as if she were about to count to ten.

One, two, three, Janey began, her lips barely forming the words, but then she hesitated. What came after that, three?

No, she'd already said three.

She could not remember the next number, so she curled up into a tight little ball on the cold desert sand, shut her eyes, and listened to her sister cry.

Janey's smile was tender. Don't worry, YoYo, she promised silently—I'll take care of you.

CHAPTER TWO

A Quick Happy Birthday

"Happy birthday, Janey," YoYo murmured, as if some-one had just told her what to say.

Jane Bishop opened her eyes cautiously.

It couldn't be her birthday. Her birthday was July sixth, and today was—well, it was days earlier than that.

And where was she, anyway? Her face was com-pletely bandaged, except for her eyes, and under a blue cotton blanket, something was squeezing each of her legs with rhythmic wheezes. It felt kind of good. "YoYo? Are you okay?"

"She's fine. I'm here, too, honey," a man's voice said. It reminded Janey of the end of *The Wizard of Oz*, when everybody gathered around Dorothy's bed.

That was Grandpa standing there. He was holding YoYo. "A lady called me the miracle child," YoYo announced. "We're staying at a motel. I get to have Cokes from the machine and everything. Let me down," she instructed her grandfather.

"Just if you promise to stay put," he told her. He set her as carefully on the shiny vinyl floor as if she were a great big sugar cookie that might break apart at any moment.

"What are you wearing?" Janey tried to ask, but it sounded more like "Whut weng," even to her. She did not like YoYo's outfit, though.

Aunt Baby must have chosen it. It was just her style, the shirt all pink and ruffly, with a cartoon character slapped on the chest and glitter decorations down each arm.

Their mother would hate it.

Mommy. Where was—

"Don't try to talk, darlin'," Grandpa said.

"Or your teeth might fall out," YoYo added helpfully.

Janey always liked it when Grandpa called her darlin'. She tried to ignore what YoYo had just said, though. YoYo had kind of a warped sense of humor for a five-year-old—but she was probably just kidding about the teeth, Janey thought, reassuring herself.

"Give Janey her birthday present, YoYo," Grandpa told the little girl.

There was a moment's silence, during which Janey could almost hear her sister trying to come up with a good reason why she should get to keep Janey's gift. YoYo hated for other people to get presents when there was nothing for her. "I think it got losted," she said, trying to sound babyish and cute.

"Yolanda."

"Oh, *okay*. Here," YoYo said, thrusting a stuffed animal—a parrot, maybe, or some other kind of color-ful bird—toward Janey's face. Janey flinched, unable to stop herself. A gift-shop tag dangled from one of the bird's fuzzy legs, but someone had crossed out the price with a thick black marker.

Janey's mother always wrapped presents properly, and she insisted that a card accompany each gift. "If we're going to bother doing it at all, we'll do it right," she often told the girls. So the stuffed animal wasn't from her.

"Thank you," Janey said, wriggling a hand up from under the covers to accept the gift. Her hands felt pretty normal, at least.

YoYo didn't let go. "Mousey burned up in the fire,"

she said, almost conversationally. Mousey was YoYo's favorite cuddle toy.

The fire. What fire?

"Yolanda," Grandpa said warningly, "I told you we were just stopping by to wish your sister a quick happy birthday. We'll have the other talk later."

The other talk.

Later.

But Janey wanted to have that talk now. "No, you guys can stay," she said. "Keep it," she told YoYo, letting go of the gift.

"Tell her to stop talking, Grandpa. She sounds dumb, and she looks scary, all wrapped up like that," YoYo said, turning away from Janey. She clutched the bird to her chest, though, and clucked lovingly at it. "I'm going to name you Birdy, yes I am. You're my little Birdy."

YoYo sounded like a cartoon mom, Janey thought, and suddenly she felt annoyed. "Shut up," she said. This came out clearly.

"You shut up," YoYo replied, not even looking at her. "Just because you got to ride in a helicopter, that doesn't make you so great."

A helicopter?

Grandpa looked a little shocked. "Now, girls," he began uncertainly.

"She's not the boss of me," YoYo said. "She's not my mom." She flipped a wisp of hair over one pink shoulder as if she'd been getting ready for this moment all her life, and she glared at Janey, ready for a fight.

"Yolanda!"

It was Janey's twelfth birthday, and she was in a private room on the second floor of Children's Hospital in Phoenix, Arizona. She knew that much, now.

There was some discussion going on about whether or not she should be in that room, however, and she was overhearing most of it.

"I really think Jane would be better off if we moved her in with a girl closer to her own age," the woman with a clipboard said to someone who must have just walked in. The clipboard woman had come just as Grandpa and YoYo were leaving. She'd been trying for an hour to get Janey to talk to her, or even to write down her thoughts, but Janey finally pretended to fall asleep.

Because whose business was it what had happened? Some stranger's?

Not that Janey could remember much about the car accident—or the day leading up to it, or the days after it.

The doctors had told her that was to be expected, though. "You've experienced a shocking event, Jane, and then there's the concussion. . . ."

She did remember a few things. Her parents had been talking softly in the front seat, and then they were laughing their private laugh, and then there were bright lights, and black sky, and there were stars whirling past the open window, and then—

"We call her Janey," an angry voice shot back. "And she is going to stay in the best private room this hospital has to offer. And that—that *woman* and her boneheaded husband are going to pay for it, every last cent!"

Aunt Baby. Janey shut her eyes tighter and wished she could turn her face to the wall. She was supposed to lie perfectly still, though.

She counted a few leg squeezes. The leggings-like devices were there to reduce the chance of her getting a blood clot, the clipboard woman had explained. There was a slight danger of this, because Janey had been lying in one position for so long.

Four days, so far.

"I know you're upset, and rightfully so," Janey heard the clipboard woman say softly, "but we really need to think of what's best for—"

"That woman thinks she can just get into a fight with her husband, Mr. Bigshot Lawyer, in Palm Springs—and then take off like a bat out of you-know-where, guzzling booze all the way back to their big fancy home in Prescott, A.Z.," Aunt Baby said, her voice shaking with rage. "But then, *bam*, she passes out and kills a couple of innocent people. And to top it all off, she probably figures she's going to get away with murder—just because of who she's married to."

Janey felt dizzy, hearing all these words at once. She could not sort them out.

"Ms. Bishop, the justice system will—"

"Oh, the justice system!" Aunt Baby interrupted again. "I'm sure the *justice system* is going to help me raise those two little girls. I'll remember to call the *justice system* whenever I need a baby-sitter. Get me their phone number, would you?"

"I only meant that—"

"If I'd wanted kids, I would have had them," Aunt Baby snapped. "Did you ever think of that?"

Janey thought her heart was going to stop beating. *Mommy. Poppy.*

"I think we should move this discussion out into the hall, don't you?" the clipboard woman said firmly.

"No, I do not," Aunt Baby snapped. "She can't hear us anyway. She's asleep."

"I don't think so," the clipboard woman said. "I believe she can hear every single word."

Criminal charges were being brought by the state of Arizona against Ronelle Sandor, the accused drunk driver.

The judge ordered that Janey be interviewed in the hospital, once her doctors gave their permission. She had been in the hospital for ten days, and her doctors finally felt that Janey had safely passed the period during which swelling of her brain might have further endangered her.

No attorneys were allowed to be present during the interview, but the small room quickly filled: a nurse sat closest to Janey, watching her for signs of distress; a court official sat opposite her bed, asking questions; a court reporter took down every word she said; and a man operating a video recorder taped the proceedings.

Since Janey was younger than fifteen years old, and since it was hoped she would be able to leave for California before long and continue her recovery there, under another doctor's supervision, this taped testimony was going to be allowed as her testimony during the criminal trial.

And so Janey learned that she could say "I can't remember!" in a dozen different ways, and people would still listen.

Everyone was very nice to her.

But they didn't make her cry, Janey thought with some satisfaction. She had wanted to avoid that, because if she cried, then everything that people were saying had happened would be true.

So in a way, it was all up to her.

CHAPTER THREE

What If

"They're going to fix you up as good as new in California," the consulting plastic surgeon said, beaming. "Maybe even better than new, but not for another couple of months. Not until your face heals. But then they'll smooth you out like nobody's business! I know grown-up ladies who would give anything to have the operation you'll be getting." He was standing half in Janey's room as he spoke and half in the hallway, as if he was supposed to be two places at once but couldn't quite figure out how to pull it off.

"How could I be better than new?" Janey managed to ask, fingering the bandages that covered the bumpy pieces of grit that had gotten embedded under her skin as she skidded across the desert floor at a million miles an hour.

The surgeon laughed as if Janey had tried to make a joke. He looked at his watch.

"I mean it," Janey insisted, not backing down. "How could any doctor make me better than my own mother and father did?"

The man paled under his tan, and he stepped back into the room, letting the heavy door close behind him. "I—I—"

"Oh, it's okay. You can go," Janey said, suddenly feeling sorry for him.

"I only meant that—that you're going to feel like a whole new person, Jane. It'll only be a little debridement. You know, touch-up work, to smooth all those abrasions and even out that cut on your cheek a bit. You're a pretty girl, honey, and we want to keep you that way."

But she didn't *want* to be touched up, Janey thought.

She didn't want to feel like a whole new person.

She just wanted things to be the way they used to be.

"What are you so worried about, Janey? They have excellent plastic surgeons in California, you know," the clipboard woman told Janey that afternoon. Her name was Ms. Ramiro, Janey had learned, and she was okay—as long as they didn't talk about the accident. But the woman seemed to have a one-track mind.

What about the way I look now? Janey wished she could shout. *Why do I have to go around scaring little kids for two more months just to make things easier for some California doctor?*

And if you must know, she wanted to add, *I'm worried about looking different. My mother and father won't be able to recognize me if that dumb plastic surgeon changes me too much.*

After they find them, I mean.

But she couldn't bring herself to utter the words.

If she said them aloud, maybe it wouldn't happen.

"How long can a person live in the desert without any food or water?" Janey asked her grandfather as casually as she could.

Grandpa looked up from his newspaper. "Darlin'," he said.

Janey made herself meet his gaze. "I was just asking, that's all. Can't a person ask questions around here?"

"Your parents are dead, Janey. Dead."

"You didn't see their bodies, did you?"

"No." The newspaper was almost bent in half, her grandfather was gripping it so hard.

"Well, what if someone made a mistake?" Janey continued, relentless. This was an argument that had circled in her brain for hours on end, and she had to ask. "YoYo and I got knocked out of the car when it flipped over, didn't we? And no one can figure out how *that* happened. What if Mommy and Poppy are still wandering around out—"

"They're dead, Janey," Grandpa repeated. "Don't make me keep saying it."

"But, Grandpa, if you didn't see their bodies, how do you know for sure that they—"

"The dentist sent down their X rays from Flagstaff."

"The *dentist*?" Janey asked, confused.

"Everyone's fillings and things are different, and they usually don't burn. That's how they identify bodies after bad car accidents," Grandpa said. He looked as if he was going to be sick.

"Oh."

That was that, then.

CHAPTER FOUR

Eeny, Meeny, Miney

Her hospital days seemed endless. The high points were when the doctors made their rounds in the morning, even though Janey was embarrassed to be the center of attention, and when the floor-waxing man whirred his machine down the hall each afternoon.

The door to her room was usually left open, no matter how many times she asked that it be closed, and the floor-waxing man always made a funny face and waved at Janey.

The other twenty-three hours each day were boring, even though Janey sometimes suddenly felt terrified for no reason that she could figure out. And occasionally there was pain. The fear or pain might only last a second or two, but even that was enough to make it difficult for Janey to let her mind relax the rest of the time. It was as if she had to keep her eyes open, or who knew what might happen?

Therefore, she was spending a lot of time thinking, but only about certain things. She attempted to reconstruct every detail of her life, for instance—of her real life with her friends in Flagstaff, that was, not this bogus Phoenix hospital life.

Losing herself in such a detailed kind of memory helped Janey to make sleepless hours pass.

It was kind of like a game, actually.

Also, thinking about her friends kept Janey from thinking about anything else.

She gazed out her hospital window at the moppy tops of the dusty palm trees that lined busy McDowell Road. Her father had given the girls their nicknames, she recalled. Ramona was known as Eeny, Janey was Meeny, and Stacy was Miney. When he saw them together, which they were most of the time, Poppy could never resist asking, "What happened to Mo?"

Eeny, Meeny, Miney, Mo. The girls pretended to hate the names, but they often used them—when they were alone.

And in a funny way, her friends' nicknames fit, Janey thought, satisfied with this idea. After all, wasn't

Ramona, "Eeny," the smallest of the three, and just about the girliest girl it was possible to be? Barely five feet tall, she had shiny black curls that tumbled casually onto her shoulders—well, the arrangement of her hair *looked* casual—and big brown eyes encircled by the longest, thickest eyelashes in Flagstaff, Arizona. Ramona Biggerstaff looked both younger and older than her twelve years.

And Ramona's voice didn't help decide the matter of her age any. Whispery-low, but still with a trace of the lisp that had plagued her when she was in primary school, that same little voice could fire off zingers that would make a stone laugh. And their teachers had never had a clue.

Ramona got a lot of mileage out of being tiny and cute.

All three of the girls lived in the old part of Flagstaff, up on the hill above Route 66 and the Amtrak station. The Biggerstaffs lived on Cherry Street, just a block down from Janey's house on Leroux. Ramona had a little brother named Ned and a baby sister named—named *something*, Janey thought, brooding suddenly.

The concussion was still having some lingering

effects, her doctors said: forgetfulness, insomnia, headache, dizziness.

Irritability. Depression.

Blah, blah, blah.

Anyway, Janey thought moodily, frowning in concentration, Ramona's bedroom was wallpapered in yellow roses. The rest of her decorating scheme was white-on-white; puffy quilts sat like clouds atop Ramona's perfectly made twin beds, and snowy dust ruffles fell to the floor like flower girls' dresses.

Ramona had even *been* a flower girl—twice! She was born for the role.

But woe to the friend who flopped down on one of those spotless beds without first removing her shoes. You practically had to take a bath before settling down to talk or listen to music in Ramona Biggerstaff's room.

Ramona would just *love* this mint-green, fake-cheerful hospital room, Janey thought with some of her old sarcasm—which had usually been appreciated, she remembered.

At least by her friends.

Camille. That was the baby sister's name.

✷ ✷ ✷

Stacy's nickname was "Miney," and that fit, too.
She was an only child, and she was spoiled rotten, the
girls—even Stacy!—cheerfully agreed. She was definitely not used to sharing, although that unattractive
quality had improved as the years passed.

"Don't forget, that's mine," she would still remind
Ramona or Janey when they borrowed a CD, however.
"I'm going to need it back for the weekend."

But she claimed she was only being cautious, and
such nagging reminders were better than the old
"Mine, mine, mine!" that had practically been Stacy's
anthem when the girls were toddlers. Janey could still
picture a scarlet-faced Stacy clutching doll clothes
and picture books to her skinny little chest, certain
that the "friends" her mother was making her play
with were going to run off with or ruin her treasures.

Stacy Lindholm lived in a big old three-story
house over on San Francisco Street, which was one
block east of Leroux. Stacy had the entire third story
to herself: a pale blue bedroom with window seats; a
wood-paneled playroom; a large dressing room; an
immense bathroom. She even had her own little
refrigerator in the playroom, and it was always well
stocked with juice boxes, bottled water, and soda.

Naturally, the third floor of the Lindholms' house

was the girls' favorite hangout. They had the most privacy there.

Janey shut her eyes and counted imaginary stairs. Were there fourteen of them leading up to the Lindholms' magical third floor?

Twelve, thirteen, *fourteen*.

Stacy was the tallest of the three girls, and the most athletic, and the gloomiest by nature. She sometimes reminded Janey of Eeyore, in the old Winnie-the-Pooh books. "Why are we even trying? We'll never finish this stupid assignment in time," she'd said just last May, right before their final group project of the semester was due. The girls were up to their elbows in papier-mâché paste in Stacy's playroom at the time, and Ramona had simultaneously been making a face at the sticky mess and fretting out loud about the state of her manicure.

But the project—a diorama of historic Flagstaff, set against the snowy San Francisco Peaks that rose like frosted cantaloupes behind the fragile little group of buildings—had gotten the girls an A-, and even Stacy was satisfied with that.

"Oh, lighten up, Miney," Janey had teased, trying to wipe a fleck of paste from her cheek with her shoulder. She wasn't too worried about making Stacy mad, because—like Eeyore—Stacy was basically kindhearted and lovable. She never held a grudge.

Stacy was pretty, too, although she didn't seem to know it. Her eyes were the most amazing blue, and she wore her dark blond hair very, very short, with even shorter wispy bangs. Janey would never have had the nerve to try to pull off a style like that. But Stacy's love of running, swimming, and tennis gave her the slender, long-muscled legs that anyone in the world would admire, and she was the kind of girl who always looked great in photographs. Perhaps that was why she was so confident.

In fact, Stacy could be a model or an actress someday, Janey was sure of it. Her friend looked a lot like those "I was so gawky and ugly!" pictures Janey was always seeing in *People*, illustrating the articles in which movie stars groaned about how terrible they used to look—when, really, the only weird thing in the picture was the person's hairstyle.

But most movie stars' "before" pictures were everyone else's hoped-for "after" pictures, didn't they realize that? With their big, expressive eyes and their wide mouths that always looked as if they were about to say something clever?

Stacy looked like one of those pictures.

In other words, she was already beautiful—only no one but Janey seemed to realize it yet.

She, Janey, was in the middle: "Meeny." Her friends called her that teasingly, though, because, according to them, she was anything but mean. If anything, they said, Janey was too nice—in public, anyway. She tried so hard to see everyone's side in an argument that she sometimes had trouble explaining *her* views—or even knowing what they were.

Janey was only that wishy-washy at school, though. With her friends or family, she was much better able to voice her opinions.

Of course, having a little sister to boss around helped Janey to assert herself at home.

Janey was "in the middle" in a number of ways: height, weight, even the length and color of her hair. Medium brown, it was cut to one length and hit the middle of her neck. She might not have Ramona's outrageous eyelashes or Stacy's big blue eyes, but Janey secretly felt that her own eyes looked interesting enough. And although she always put down plain old "brown" on forms she had to fill out, her eyes were flecked with a gold that made them extraordinary.

Or so her mother had always claimed.

Mommy.

Janey shifted uncomfortably in her hospital bed, then focused her thoughts on trivia once more.

Her eyebrows had a naturally pretty shape—thank goodness, she sometimes thought, because she couldn't imagine pulling little hairs out of her head just to look better. And her lashes, while not in Ramona Biggerstaff's league, were perfectly respectable.

Ramona and Stacy often praised Janey, telling her, for instance, that she had the best complexion of any girl in the sixth grade. "And I mean of all the sixth grades in the entire state of Arizona!" Ramona had added once, in her usual extravagant way.

"Have you *ever* broken out?" Stacy asked, peering at her own temporarily blotchy chin in the mirror.

Janey laughed, feeling pleased but self-conscious. "Your face is going to clear up, but I'll never be tall like you."

"And we'll never be as smart as you," Stacy shot back.

Ramona nodded in agreement, but she didn't look too disturbed by this admission. "That's not why we like you, though," she said. "We like you because you're so comfy to be with."

"Yeah," Stacy said, grinning. "You're fairly low-maintenance."

The three friends often complimented each other, sometimes teasingly and sometimes with shy sincerity. They liked to make each other feel good—without ever getting goopy about things. The point was, they were best friends, and they had been forever. Other kids quarreled, split up, and formed new alliances, but not Janey, Ramona, and Stacy.

They were like puzzle pieces that fit together.

And Janey had thought they always would.

Pretty soon it would be time for her steam-warmed dinner; Janey could tell without even looking at the big wall clock in her room. The nurses kicked back and relaxed just before the carts were wheeled onto their floor, and even the noisy kid down the hall quieted down.

In fact, the entire hospital seemed to pause to take a breath.

Janey took a breath, too.

It was time.

She brought the back of her bed up as high as it would go, then sat up even straighter and swung her legs—free of the squeezing machine, now—over the side of the bed.

She wasn't supposed to get out of bed unless there was a nurse in the room, but *tough*. She was going to go into the bathroom—all by herself, for once.

Because Janey wanted to look at her face in the mirror, not merely to glimpse a tiny part of her reflection in a nurse's glasses as Silvadene cream was reapplied to her wounds and the nonstick bandages were changed.

No, Janey wanted a real look. She would take off every bandage, if she had to. Who cared what the doctors and nurses might say or do when they found out?

What more could possibly hurt her?

CHAPTER FIVE

Visitors

"You have visitors coming," Ms. Ramiro said to Janey the next day, stepping into the room.

The floor-waxing guy had just whirred by. *Take a good look, while you're at it!* Janey wanted to shout when he'd peeked in at her.

Visitors. Janey touched her rebandaged face. It had looked even worse than she'd thought it might. But who cared? What difference did it make, considering?

"Who?" Janey asked listlessly. "Grandpa? Aunt Baby?" Really, she wondered, why was Ms. Ramiro bothering her with such useless announcements? Because Grandpa crept into her room—or Aunt Baby barged in—every single day. They took turns, because one of them always had to stay behind at the motel to entertain YoYo.

"No," Ms. Ramiro said. "Your friends are coming.

Stacy Lindholm and—and Ramona Biggerstaff," she said, checking her clipboard. "I told Stacy's mom it was okay when she called earlier this morning. They're driving down from Flagstaff now."

Stacy. And. Ramona.

Suddenly, Janey cared about her face—and she almost hated her old friends for making her feel this way. "But—but they can't come," she said, struggling to sit up in bed. "You can't decide that for me. They belong in Flagstaff!"

"Hang on a sec," Ms. Ramiro said, hurrying to Janey's side. Her round face looked concerned as she pressed the button that would raise the hospital bed to sitting position. "There. Comfy?" she asked, inadvertently using one of Ramona's favorite words.

"No, I'm not *comfy*," Janey said, trying to control her temper. "Would you be comfy if you were me? I look like a freak, like a mummy! I don't want my friends seeing me like this."

"You don't look like a freak, Janey," Ms. Ramiro said soothingly. "And people expect bandages when they visit someone in a hospital."

"I'm not talking about that," Janey snapped. "I'm talking about what's underneath the bandages!" Yesterday's reflected image from her bathroom mirror's unbreakable metallic surface seemed suddenly to hover before her eyes: wall-to-wall disaster on her cheeks, forehead, and nose, those wounds still meaty, pitted, and red, since the doctors didn't want them to scab; the green leftover smudges of the bruises she'd suffered banging into the desert floor; and, to top it all off, tiny black Frankenstein-style stitching along one jawbone.

Any random scrap of skin she could see glowed almost scarlet, and the most damaged parts of her face had been covered with plastic wrap, as if she were some gruesome leftover.

Well, maybe she *was* a leftover. A leftover Bishop.

Only her eyes had looked normal. Horrified, but normal.

"Don't lie to me! Don't forget, I know what I look like!" Janey practically howled.

"Oh, Janey—you should have told me you wanted to see your face. We could have arranged something," Ms. Ramiro said, taking one of Janey's cold hands between her own.

"*It's my face*," Janey shouted. "It's not like I need a hall pass to go visit it!" She snatched her fingers away from Ms. Ramiro, although really, she had enjoyed being touched—by someone other than a doctor or a nurse.

What they did wasn't really like touching. It was more like prodding.

"Of course it's your face. And when it's time for plastic surgery, you'll come through with flying colors, I just know it," Ms. Ramiro said, darting over to close Janey's heavy door.

Oh, great, Janey thought—*now* she was getting some privacy.

"The doctors are very optimistic that your face will be as good as new in a few months, Janey. I wouldn't lie to you about this," Ms. Ramiro said, dragging a chair to Janey's bedside and sitting down.

"You would too."

"I would not. Ask me anything."

"Okay," Janey said, her anger giving her courage. "Will there be scars?"

"Maybe, but the doctors hope that they'll be minimal. And they'll operate again, if there's any real problem. Next question."

"Well," Janey said, thinking fast, "how long *exactly* until they can fix me up?"

"They can't say. It won't be for another six weeks, probably," Ms. Ramiro said. "See, the body heals in unpredictable ways, they tell me. And some parts of your face that look bad now may end up not needing any surgery at all. But you won't have to stay in the hospital six more weeks. You'll be ready to go home in a few days, in fact."

Home.

To her credit, Ms. Ramiro blushed almost as soon as she'd said the word. "I'm sorry, Janey," she said softly. "I meant, you'll be ready to leave the hospital."

"All bandaged up like this?"

"You'll be able to take the bandages off and get some fresh air from time to time at—when you're in California," Ms. Ramiro said, stumbling to correct herself. "As long as you don't let any scabs form, you should be okay, but that's what the cream is for."

"They don't have fresh air in Glendale. They have smog," Janey said, remembering.

"Even so," Ms. Ramiro said, smiling her encouragement at what she thought was Janey's little joke.

Janey thought for a moment. "How come the rest of my skin is so red? Even the part that's not all chewed up?"

"I don't know," Ms. Ramiro said promptly. "Do you want me to ask the doctor for you?"

"Ask him if the red will fade," Janey said, looking down at her lonely hands.

"Okay," Ms. Ramiro said, making a note. "But I'm

sure it will. I've seen lots of these cases before."

"You've seen cases where a kid was hurt so much that she had to have plastic surgery?" Janey asked.

Ms. Ramiro nodded, her dark eyes serious.

"Where a kid's mom and dad were killed in the middle of the night by a drunk driver?"

Ms. Ramiro nodded again, but just barely.

"Where a kid had to move in with people she barely knows? And take care of her little sister, no matter what?"

Ms. Ramiro bit her lips together, but she nodded again. "I have seen that before, Janey. Unfortunately. Not that it makes things any easier for *you*."

Janey shrugged. "You've probably seen lots of worse stuff, even," she said. "So don't worry about me. Just— just tell everyone to leave me alone, okay? Because I don't want any visitors. I mean, I'm sorry Mrs. Lindholm had to drive all this way and everything, but I *don't*. So you can tell them to just go home."

"Too late, I'm afraid," Ms. Ramiro said, watching Janey's door swing open.

Ramona's face paled when she first saw Janey.

"Trick or treat," Janey snapped.

"Oh, come on—you don't look so bad," Stacy said

as she and her mom followed Ramona into the hospital room. But Stacy had begun uttering those reassuring words before even seeing her, Janey noticed. Now Stacy seemed to be her gloomy old self, as if she were thinking, *This is worse than I thought!*

Mrs. Lindholm looked as though she was about to start crying. In fact, she was ready in advance, handkerchief in hand.

Eighty percent of my face is bandaged up like a mummy's, Janey thought bitterly, *and I don't look so bad? What did I look like before, then?*

"I'm Linda Ramiro. We spoke over the phone," Ms. Ramiro said to Mrs. Lindholm, taking charge. She shook hands first with Mrs. Lindholm, then with Stacy and Ramona.

"Hello," Mrs. Lindholm said, her voice faint. She dabbed at her eyes—already reddened—with the crumpled handkerchief.

"Why don't we step into the hall and give these girls a chance to catch up?" Ms. Ramiro said, taking Mrs. Lindholm firmly by the elbow and leading her to the door.

"You can stay," Janey called out, but they were already gone, and she was left alone with Ramona and Stacy.

Eeny and Miney, about a hundred years ago.

"You really don't look that terrible," Stacy said, pulling up a chair.

"You don't," Ramona echoed, a second too late.

"It's no big deal," Janey told them. "I don't even care *what* I look like."

Ramona and Stacy exchanged quick, panicked glances, then Stacy cleared her throat. "We're really sorry about your mom and dad."

Janey almost hated her for saying that, because "sorry" *so* didn't cover it.

"Sorry" was for when you banged your bike into someone's trash can.

"Sorry" was for an embarrassing burp at the dinner table.

It wasn't for a mother and a father killed in a crash and then burned up so badly that it took a dentist to identify them.

And Poppy had hated going to the dentist!

"That's okay," Janey said, sensing how awkward her friend must be feeling. "Thank you," she added formally, knowing by now that this was the expected response.

But really, Janey asked herself suddenly, what was her *true* response?

She was—*embarrassed*, she realized, horrified.

She was embarrassed that underneath the bandages, her face looked so gross and pathetic. She was embarrassed that her greasy bangs were poking out between strips of bandage like some goofy fringe.

She was embarrassed at the cow pajamas she was wearing, which had been a joke Valentine's Day gift from her mom, really, but which happened to be what Grandpa had grabbed out of the drawer back home in Flagstaff. Embarrassed at the spoonful of milk and cornflakes she'd spilled down the front of one black and white cow earlier in the morning.

She was embarrassed that her parents were dead.

How could I even think that? Janey asked herself, appalled.

Because now I'm different, came her own answer. *And that will never change.*

"YoYo's picture was in the paper," Ramona announced, trying to change the subject as she perched on the arm of Stacy's chair. "She looked so-o-o cute."

"Oh, great," Janey said, groaning. "She'll be even worse to live with than before. If that's even possible."

"Is she really okay?" Stacy asked, her blue eyes seeming to darken with concern.

"I thought you could barely stand YoYo," Janey said coolly.

Stacy jerked back in her pink vinyl chair as if she'd been slapped, and Janey felt a small thrill of—of relief, she thought, surprised.

Now someone else was hurting, too. And that felt *good*.

"I never said that. I *like* YoYo," Stacy objected.

"She does like her, Janey," Ramona confirmed, sounding almost as though she were telling the truth. "She says so all the time."

"Since when?" Janey asked in a tone meant to inform the others that she did not expect an answer.

Ramona and Stacy exchanged looks again, and in that moment, Janey realized that the three girls' friendship had changed—probably forever. Now Ramona and Stacy were friends, and she, Janey, would become what's-her-name, that bad-luck kid who'd moved to California.

Ramona and Stacy probably wouldn't even talk about her much, just in case all that misfortune was contagious.

They would make friends with whatever new girl moved into her house, into her room.

Janey *hated* Ramona and Stacy, come to think of

it. "How do you like my complexion now?" she asked Ramona, touching icy fingers to the reddened bit of skin around her eyes that was showing. "Is it still the best in Arizona?"

Ramona sat up straight and scowled. "You're not being very nice, Janey."

"Shhh," Stacy warned Ramona, looking worried.

"Oh, let her talk," Janey said. "In fact, let's hear her make a joke. You're good at that, Ramona — so, say something funny."

"You are so *messed up*," Ramona said, getting to her feet.

"Well, duh!" Janey said, a sick, light feeling flooding her chest.

They were about to leave. She just knew it.

"I'm leaving," Ramona said, confirming Janey's prediction. Ramona stalked out the door. She even tried to slam it behind her, but hospital doors don't slam.

Janey almost felt like laughing out loud.

"Congratulations," Stacy said sarcastically. "I guess you really showed *her*."

"Well, why don't you leave, too?" Janey said. "Go back home to your mother, and your father, and all your *stuff*, including your own private refrigerator."

"You're one of my two best friends, Janey," Stacy said, not budging. "And it's only a small refrigerator, you dope."

"I *was* one of your friends. And don't call me names."

"Why are you acting so weird? Is it because you banged your head?"

I don't know, Janey wanted to cry out. *Maybe it's because I want to get this breakup over with.*

"Janey?"

"I'm tired of talking," Janey said. "I want you to leave."

Forever, she added silently, closing her eyes.

When she opened them again, the room was empty.

CHAPTER SIX

This Isn't About the Money

"Now, there are going to be reporters outside, and maybe even TV cameras," Aunt Baby said, excited. "Coverage," she added, summing it up. She inspected her face in the hospital room's tiny mirror and smacked her lips together once.

She was wearing more makeup than she usually did. Her eyebrows looked as though they'd been stenciled on by someone using a kit.

"Oh, Irene, give it a rest," Grandpa said. "You're starting to talk like one of *them*."

"Can I wear some lipstick, too?" YoYo asked Aunt Baby. She pushed her lips out as far as they would go, in preparation. She was wearing a white dress, white socks, and white shoes. She looked ridiculous, in Janey's opinion—like a giant moth.

Aunt Baby had started dressing YoYo entirely in

white the same day a second person had called her a miracle child. "Two times and it's a trend," Aunt Baby said. YoYo's picture had appeared in the newspaper three more times since then, and that was only in Arizona. There were rumors about a magazine article, too; Aunt Baby told anyone who would listen that she was "in negotiations."

"You couldn't negotiate your way out of a paper bag," Grandpa joked.

"Just a little lipstick?" YoYo wheedled.

"A dab," Aunt Baby agreed, laughing. She touched the center of YoYo's lips with some coral-colored lipstick.

They were both just totally into this, Janey thought, disgusted.

She had wanted simply to check out of the hospital and leave, and Grandpa had backed her up on this—until he'd talked with their lawyer, Mr. Chesterton, retained to bring civil suit against the drunk driver on behalf of Janey and YoYo after the criminal proceedings ended. Mr. Chesterton said it was vital for the girls' interests for people to be reminded of what had happened to them.

And she, Janey, was to be the lawyer's number one visual aid, she realized.

"Want some lipstick, Janey?" Aunt Baby asked, turning around. She held up the golden lipstick as if it were a yummy snack.

Janey looked up from where she sat in her wheelchair. "No, thanks," she said, putting as much unspoken meaning as she dared into the two words.

"She's fine exactly the way she is," Grandpa said, which infuriated Janey for some reason. Now she wanted to grab Aunt Baby's lipstick and smear it all over her bandaged face.

She'd like to see what the TV cameras made of that!

"Don't get any lipstick on your dress, YoYo," Aunt Baby said, fussing over the little girl's sash.

"But I wanted Janey to wear lipstick, too," YoYo said, her face clouding up. "Then we'd all match."

"I changed my mind," Aunt Baby said, as if the whole thing was up to her. "It's better if she doesn't wear any, I think."

Grandpa threw up his hands. "Oh, for pete's sake." He had been short-tempered for a week, ever since the funeral in Flagstaff for Janey's parents. He was the only family member to have attended; Aunt Baby stayed behind in Phoenix with YoYo.

Janey's family's house on Leroux Street had

already been emptied out by family friends and was on the market, Aunt Baby had told her. So there was no reason to go back home. No one had wanted them to have to do that.

Home. Janey guessed her home was in California, now.

But she couldn't even remember what Grandpa's house looked like.

"Let's go," she said, looking around the familiar room one last time. All the cards and photos that had accumulated over the past days had been taken off her bulletin board and jammed into a brand-new pink scrapbook that had *Memories* written across the front in gold script. As if she would want to remember! "I'm ready," she repeated. "Why can't we just go outside and get it over with?"

We have to wait for Mr. Chesterton," Aunt Baby said, looking out of the window. Arnold Chesterton was her new hero.

"I don't see why we have to wait," Grandpa muttered, checking the drawers once again for anything they might have left behind.

Aunt Baby's eyes shone. "He told us to, for one thing. I think he'll probably want to make a statement to the press before introducing the girls. And I might have something to add, if he thinks it's a good idea." She returned to the mirror to check her lipstick once more, and she fluffed her steel-gray hair. Janey didn't know for sure how old Aunt Baby was; sixty-two or sixty-three, she thought.

YoYo twirled around on the shiny floor a couple of times. "The miracle child has to go potty," she announced loudly.

Grandpa snorted. "Better ask Mr. Chesterton's permission first, before you pee," he said, and Janey couldn't help but laugh.

"But I can't wait!"YoYo squawked.

"He was only teasing," Aunt Baby said, shooting Grandpa a look as she hustled YoYo into the bathroom.

"And stop calling yourself the miracle child, YoYo," Janey called after them. "It sounds totally dumb."

"She can call herself that until after the press conference," Aunt Baby said from behind the bathroom door.

"You just wish it was you, that's all!"YoYo yelled. "I didn't even get one little cut, and you have to sit there in a wheelchair, all wrapped up like a big old dummy. A dummy mummy," she added, sounding pleased with the rhyme.

"I can walk," Janey yelled back. "It's just a stupid rule that you have to leave the hospital in a wheelchair, that's all."

"And it's only until after the press conference," Grandpa said, echoing Aunt Baby as he made a sympathetic face at Janey.

"And so naturally," Mr. Chesterton said, "we will eventually be seeking compensation on behalf of these two brave little girls." He looked down sadly as he said these last few words, and adjusted his cuffs.

Compensation meant money, Janey had learned. If Mrs. Sandor was found guilty in the criminal trial, she would be punished by the state of Arizona for breaking its laws. Grandpa and Aunt Baby said that she should have to pay a serious penalty for killing Peter and Norris Bishop, though. That amount would be determined in the civil trial, a separate lawsuit.

But *what* amount? What were a mother and father worth? Janey's head started aching again whenever she thought about this. What if some judge asked her to add up all the things Mommy and Poppy had done for her—and to put a price on them?

✴ ✴ ✴

- *Helping me with my spelling list: $5 each time.*
- *Driving me to school (without complaining) when I slept late: $3 each time.*
- *Making me feel better whenever someone hurt my feelings: $14 each time.*
- *Fixing scrambled eggs just the way I like them: $1.50 each time.*
- *Loving me, no matter what: $???*

An unforgiving late July sun beat down on the two groups of people assembled on the zigzag-patterned bricks in the hospital's desert garden, and a fountain burbled nearby, as if its brave efforts might cool things off. The first group consisted of Janey's nurses and doctors, smiling gamely for the cameras but thinking of all the other things they were supposed to be doing; a still-bandaged Janey in her wheelchair; a fidgety YoYo; Aunt Baby and Grandpa; and Mr. and Mrs. Frank Benning, Frank Benning having been the bystander who'd been slightly injured in the rescue attempt.

And then there was Janey's lawyer, Mr. Chesterton, who wasn't even sweating.

The second group was a tangle of various camera

operators and reporters who looked as though they were about to start shouting out their questions so they could pack up and leave.

A sharp glance from Mr. Chesterton sent Aunt Baby tripping over to the microphone. She tapped at it with a newly polished fingernail, though the mike had clearly been working fine only a minute earlier. She blew into it loudly, and a couple of reporters groaned. "We can hear you, lady," one of them shouted.

Janey shut her eyes halfway, dreading what was to come next.

"Testing, testing," Aunt Baby said, her mouth practically glued to the microphone. Mr. Chesterton glided over to where she was standing and murmured something in her ear. "Okay," she told him, and her voice boomed out over the cactuses and pitted black lava rock that encircled them. "I'm Irene Bishop," she began, "and this is my brother, Howard," she added, gesturing vaguely toward Grandpa, who raised one hand.

YoYo broke away from his grasp and started twirling. Her skirt lifted, revealing a fluffy white petticoat. Cameras flashed, and some reporters laughed encouragingly.

"Did you see any angels out there in the desert, Yolanda?" one of them shouted.

"Yes, I did," YoYo said, her voice surprisingly strong. "One of them let me wear her badge and play with the siren, too. But she was hiding her wings."

More laughter. "This is pure gold," Janey heard one man say.

"YoYo," Janey muttered, groaning. Really, her little sister was sickening. And all those cameras egging her on weren't helping things any.

Their parents had just hated stuff like this.

After giving everyone a chance to get a picture, Mr. Chesterton clamped his well-manicured hand onto YoYo's shoulder, and she practically went limp. He walked her back to Grandpa.

Aunt Baby tried again. "We're the girls' legal guardians now," she said, still standing too close to the microphone, "and it's up to us to do right by them. These little girls are brave, like Mr. Chesterton just said, but they've lost their mommy and daddy forever and ever." Her voice grew wobbly. "It's a miracle the whole family wasn't killed."

Janey stared hard at a particularly weird-looking cactus and heard YoYo start to cry.

Her little sister hadn't cried in public before now, not that Janey knew of, anyway, but Aunt Baby had let slip a complaint about YoYo's nighttime crying jags. "Anything can set her off," she'd told Janey. "If she can't find one of her toys, she cries. If she doesn't get a joke on TV, it's *boo-hoo-hoo*. The people in the room next to us pounded on the wall last night, she was sobbing so loudly when I told her that she had to have a shampoo. I thought they were going to call protective services on us!"

There was a murmur of sympathy when the reporters spotted YoYo's tears, and there were more camera flashes. Janey wanted to leap out of her wheelchair and calm her weeping sister with a hug, but she didn't want anyone to take a picture of *that*.

Aunt Baby cleared her throat into the microphone, as if hoping it might draw everyone's attention back to her. "So yes, we're going to sue," she continued, her voice growing stronger. "But this isn't about the money. It's about justice, that's all! Justice for these two wonderful children. These courageous orphans," she added dramatically—going a little over the top, in Janey's opinion.

CHAPTER SEVEN

Crossroads

The beginning of the daylong drive to California was a nightmare, at least for Janey. They traveled on Interstate 10, a huge freeway that headed almost due west—all the way to the beach, Grandpa said enticingly. They would not pass the scene of the accident, since Janey's mom and dad had been zigzagging their way down smaller roads from Flagstaff before they'd been hit on Route 60. They would have linked up with the interstate in another half hour, but they liked driving on less-traveled roads when they could, even at night, and they'd been trying to avoid Phoenix traffic.

Grandpa drove, and Aunt Baby sat next to him, finger jammed as firmly on the map as though they were wending their way down the Amazon in a canoe rather than taking the only freeway west from

Phoenix. Janey and a still-excited YoYo were in the backseat, buckled in so tightly that YoYo said her legs were tingly.

Aunt Baby was grouchy the first part of the trip. "I refuse to call it an accident," she muttered to Grandpa, but Janey heard every word. "Is it an accident if some stupid woman gets drunk—on purpose—while she's behind the wheel of a car?"

Grandpa fiddled with his cruise control but didn't say anything.

"Is it?"

"Oh," Grandpa said politely. "I just figured you were talking to yourself, Irene, you've been down that road so often."

"What road?" YoYo asked, kicking the back of Grandpa's seat.

"Quit it," Grandpa said mildly.

"He was only kidding, sugarplum," Aunt Baby called, without turning around. "That's just your grandpa's peculiar sense of humor."

It was another hot day, of course, but Grandpa's car was air-conditioned. Janey turned away from her sister before YoYo could pick some bogus fight, and she rested her forehead on cool window glass. She stared out at the desert as it whizzed by and tried not to think about Ramona and Stacy, who were probably having a really good time right about now.

How *had* she and YoYo been thrown to safety the night they'd been hit? She could only remember a few things about that night, but nothing that had happened right before that woman drifted over the center line.

Except—except for hearing her mother laugh once, that low chuckle she shared only with her husband, and seeing her reach over to caress the back of Poppy's neck as he drove.

Don't start crying, Janey told herself.

"I don't want to be a poor little orphan," YoYo finally mumbled, kicking at Grandpa's seat once more—but stopping short of actual contact.

"Well," Janey said, softly enough so that Grandpa and Aunt Baby couldn't hear, "maybe you'll be a rich little orphan by the time Mr. Chesterton gets done with things. Will that make you feel any better?"

"No."

"Me either. So shut up."

"You shut up."

YoYo had a flat-out tantrum at the McDonald's in Blythe, the first California town on the other side of the Colorado River. Aunt Baby had rushed into the rest room, almost knocking down an old lady using a walker, so Janey was left standing in line with her sister while Grandpa tried to stake out a table for them all.

Janey was so embarrassed by her still-bandaged face that she'd begged to be allowed to stay in the car, but Grandpa said it was way too hot out for that. She would have refused to come in anyway, she thought, furious, if she'd known she was going to be abandoned in line with YoYo.

People were staring at her.

Even though it was mid-afternoon, the place was crowded—mostly for the air-conditioning and the attached two-story play area, Janey suspected, although the smell of French fries was making her stomach growl in spite of everything.

It had been ages since she'd had any normal food, and she began planning what she would order with an enthusiasm that surprised her. "I don't wanna wait," YoYo said, yanking at her sash until it came undone and trailed on the sticky tile floor.

The miracle-child dress was looking a little droopy, Janey noted with satisfaction. "You have to wait."

"But I don't wanna."

"Well, you hafta," Janey whispered, blushing

underneath her bandages. "Grandpa and Aunt Baby will probably let you play in the climbing structure after lunch, if you're good."

"Everyone should let us go first," YoYo said loudly. The man standing in front of them looked back at them, amused, and then—getting a look at Janey—concerned. "Stop staring at me," YoYo yelled. "I'm an orphan!"

Several people were watching them by now, Janey noticed, mute with embarrassment. She ducked her head so that her hair swung over her bandaged face a little, hiding the few red patches that remained visible. She hoped no one would figure out who they were, although there had been lots of "coverage," as Aunt Baby put it. Newspaper articles, and so on.

"I'm hungry," YoYo whined.

"You can have these, sweetheart," a woman said, taking a super-sized sack of fries from her tray and handing them to YoYo. She gave Janey a sympathetic look.

"Please don't give her that," Janey heard herself say. "My mom and dad don't allow her to take food from strangers."

"But *I'm* not a stranger," the woman said, drawing back a little. She looked hurt.

"And we don't even have a mom and dad," YoYo said, cradling the fries. She crammed a few into her mouth and then licked salt off her fingers.

"You are acting so spoiled," Janey told her angrily. "Mommy and Poppy would be ashamed of you."

That's when the tantrum started. A full-blown hissy fit, Poppy would have called it—right before he marched YoYo's little booty right out of the restaurant, slam-dunking her hamburger into the nearest trash bin. "If anyone gets to act like a brat in this family, it's going to be me," he always joked.

Instead, Aunt Baby emerged from the rest room, rushed over to YoYo, who by now was kicking and crying on the floor, scooped her up, and glared at Janey. "What happened? What did you do?" she asked accusingly.

"She hurted my feelings," YoYo sobbed, using the baby talk that had worked so well for her in the recent past.

"I'm going out to the car," Janey said. "I feel a little bit dizzy, I think."

"But you can't leave, it's almost our turn," YoYo said, wiping away a few tears and urging Aunt Baby forward with her heels as though she were a big gray horse.

"Let her go," Aunt Baby said soothingly to YoYo.

"We can bring her something to eat in the car. Better go get the key from Grandpa, Miss Jane. And be sure to roll down the windows."

Miss Jane. Mommy's pet name for her. "Please don't call me that ever again," Janey said, as politely as she could, before turning away from them to search for Grandpa.

She was going to have to do something about YoYo, Janey thought, finishing the last cold French fry and washing it down with a final noisy slurp from her vanilla milk shake.

"Stop showing off," YoYo mumbled as more of the desert sped by.

She was sucking her thumb and twirling her hair again, Janey noticed uneasily. She thought their mother had just about cured her of those habits, too. "I'm not showing off. And stop sucking your thumb, YoYo. What are you, a baby?"

"Yeah," YoYo said from around her thumb. She twisted the hair above her ear into a coil, as if she were winding herself up.

Janey sighed and stared out of the car window once more. She was going to have her work cut out for her, she thought moodily. But if Aunt Baby was going to go stuffing her little sister's face every time she started yelling, and if Grandpa went along with everything just to keep the peace, then it was going to be up to her to teach YoYo some manners.

The way Mommy and Poppy would have wanted.

"Stop twirling your hair," she said softly.

But YoYo had fallen asleep.

Two hours later, Janey opened her eyes to see a stack of freeways up ahead, three or four layers high. And yet there didn't seem to be any cities around. "Where are we, Grandpa?" she asked quietly, so as not to wake her sister, who had curled up with her tousled head in Janey's lap.

"Just outside San Bernardino, darlin'," he told her over the gentle buzz of Aunt Baby's snore. "We'll be home in a little over an hour."

So, Janey thought, craning her neck to look up at a massive overpass as Grandpa's car roared through the deepening gloom, this weird place—right here!— was going to serve as a kind of crossroads for her. Because it was as though Arizona had been a great big magnet, and under this overpass she'd just broken free of its pull.

No more desert-garden press conference.

No more hospital, with someone always bursting into her room.

No more Flagstaff, no more house, and no more pretty bedroom all to herself, either, because at Grandpa's house, she'd be sharing a room with spoiled-rotten YoYo.

No more Stacy and Ramona.

Strangest of all, no more Mommy and Poppy.

And yet, Janey thought, it seemed as though her parents were still with her.

YoYo cried out, dreaming, and Janey rubbed her back until she quieted down.

Their mother used to do that, she remembered drowsily, and her own back ached to be touched.

The dusty car pulled into the driveway just after ten P.M. Exhausted from the long drive, Grandpa emerged stiffly from the driver's seat and gave a few experimental stretches. "Good to be home," he announced uncertainly.

The neighborhood lawns glowed gray under buzzing streetlights.

"Mercy," Aunt Baby said, struggling to unclasp her seat belt. "It doesn't look as though the Fullers remembered to water the grass twice a week like I asked."

"We can give it a good soaking tomorrow," Grandpa told her. He knocked playfully on YoYo's car window, but she was still sleeping. She had drooled a little on Janey's leg, but Janey hadn't wanted to risk waking her. *Come on out*, Grandpa beckoned to Janey.

Just a minute, Janey mimed back, holding up her index finger. Then she pointed down at YoYo, as if explaining silently to Grandpa why she was still sitting in the car.

But she didn't know why she was still sitting in the car. Not really.

CHAPTER EIGHT
Eucalyptus Terrace

Howard Bishop, Janey and YoYo's grandfather, had lived in Glendale on Eucalyptus Terrace for twenty-five years as a married man. He and his wife moved there with Peter, their only child, in 1966, when Peter was a rambunctious one-year-old. Peter Bishop—Janey and YoYo's Poppy—was thirty-six when he died in the crash; Norrie Bishop was thirty-five.

After Janey's grandmother died in 1990, Howard's sister Irene, Aunt Baby, moved in. It was a big enough house, and she had been living alone for years. Howard Bishop wasn't much of a cook, after all, and he was lonely, even though he filled as many hours as he could running his plumbing-supply business. But the business almost ran itself, as he was fond of saying.

So it made sense for Aunt Baby to move in with Grandpa.

They got along pretty well. She liked to cook and putter in the garden, and he liked to eat and look at the flowers when he wasn't at work.

Almost everyone called her Baby, and he usually did, too, except when he was angry with her. Then it was Irene. But Baby had always been her nickname; she was a surprise last addition to a family consisting of three boys.

She was much spoiled as a girl—and she intended to keep things that way, she liked to joke.

Janey and YoYo grew up calling her Aunt Baby without thinking anything of it, but Janey wondered about the name now, as she shifted her hip over the rigid bar that ran across the middle of the sofa bed in her grandfather's study. This was to be the girls' room. "We'll get bunk beds this week," Grandpa had promised, tucking them in for what was left of the night after a quick supper of tomato soup and grilled cheese sandwiches.

"Great," Janey mumbled. Yeah, she fumed silently, bunk beds were great—if you were a cowboy, or a six-year-old kid, preferably a boy. She tried not to think about the twin beds—ideal for sleepovers—in her old room in Flagstaff. She'd even gotten to choose the bedspreads for them.

Her bedroom had been almost perfect. On the second floor, and overlooking the backyard, she could play her music loud without bothering anyone. Poppy had turned one whole wall into a giant bulletin board that Janey'd almost completely covered with *stuff*, and he'd painted the other three walls violet—twice, so as to get the color exactly right.

Everything in that room had been just the way she liked it.

Bunk beds. They'd probably be decorated with bucking broncos, or something.

Next to her, YoYo moaned in her sleep.

She found her thumb, though, and quieted down.

Wide awake, Janey let her thoughts drift back to Aunt Baby. She *was* kind of babyish, in a way. Though her hair was gray, it swung loose and shiny in a short straight cut that ended just about even with her ears, and she had long bangs, as straight as they could be. Janey had seen her trim them once; Aunt Baby stretched tape across them, and then snipped away any shaggy hair that had dared to dip below the tape.

Aunt Baby was round like a baby, too. Not downright fat, but round. "I'm too good a cook, that's all," she liked to say with a laugh, patting her stomach. Grandpa was able to eat and eat without ever gaining any weight, which seemed to infuriate Aunt Baby. "Have some more of this," she'd say challengingly, sawing off another slice of her famous triple-chocolate cake.

"Don't mind if I do," Grandpa would tell her.

Poppy had been skinny, too.

She hated this room, Janey thought angrily. She hated this *house*.

That wasn't really true. Janey and YoYo had visited the two-story house on Eucalyptus Terrace every year since they'd been born. It had always seemed like a fairy-tale house to Janey—a big version of the Hansel and Gretel cottage, perhaps, only not scary. Its cream-colored stucco walls were topped by a steeply pitched dark brown shingled roof, and matching red rose bushes marched along the front of the house in a precise row. A thick pad of grass sloped gently to the street. The whole thing looked like one of YoYo's better paintings, Janey thought.

She hadn't minded visiting, but she'd never thought she would have to live here.

There was no choice, though. Her mother's parents had died when Norrie was in college, and, like Poppy, she'd been an only child.

Janey's stomach seemed to drop. What if something happened to Grandpa and Aunt Baby? Who would she and YoYo live with then?

Janey took off her bandages the next morning. She looked at herself in the bathroom mirror and tried not to feel anything at all as she gingerly patted some Silvadene onto her face.

She didn't look terrible, but she didn't look like herself. She was too red and shiny in places, and the worst, bumpiest parts of her face had definitely not healed yet.

"You've got circles under your eyes," was Aunt Baby's only comment at breakfast, to Janey's relief.

"I couldn't get to sleep."

YoYo looked up from the comics, and her mouth fell open as she saw her big sister's unbandaged face for the first time. She looked frightened.

"YoYo wouldn't *let* me sleep," Janey amended, before YoYo could say anything about her appearance.

"It's not my fault," YoYo said softly, not taking her eyes from Janey's face. "You were hogging the covers. Are you always going to look like that?"

"No, she's not," Aunt Baby said.

"But can't you cover it up?" YoYo asked Janey, pleading, almost hypnotized.

"I will after breakfast. Why? Do I look that bad?"

"No, of course not," Aunt Baby said.

"Yes," YoYo said at the same time. She looked down, blinking hard a couple of times as if trying to force back tears, and began piling jam on a piece of toast with an abandon that would have shocked their mother, Janey thought.

"Eat your toast, YoYo," Aunt Baby said unnecessarily, sliding a fried egg onto Janey's plate.

"Yeah, if you can fit it into your mouth," Janey said softly. "Where's Grandpa?" she asked Aunt Baby, before YoYo could say anything.

"He got up early and went in to work," Aunt Baby said, sitting down and pouring herself a second cup of coffee. "Now, I want to talk to you girls about something," she said, leaning forward confidentially.

Uh-oh, Janey thought. She resisted the urge to touch her face, at which YoYo was now sneaking horrified, curious peeks.

"Your grandpa's not a young man," Aunt Baby began.

"He's an old man," YoYo said, suddenly pitching into this new conversation with enthusiasm.

Aunt Baby looked startled. After all, she was a mere two years younger than her brother Howard.

"Not old, exactly," she said. "Just sixty-five, his next birthday." This was added as if it might convince the girls of Grandpa's youthfulness.

It seemed to Janey that Aunt Baby had lost the thread of her argument. "You were telling us that Grandpa's not a young man," she said.

"Oh, right. Well, he's not."

YoYo chewed thoughtfully for a moment. "Okay," she finally said, smiling.

"He was thinking about retiring," Aunt Baby continued. "Even though I was never quite sure how I'd like having him underfoot all day long," she added, mostly to herself.

But it was his house, Janey thought. Why shouldn't Grandpa retire if he wanted to?

"All that's off now, of course," Aunt Baby said, stirring her coffee moodily.

"How come?" Janey asked. "Because of us, I suppose," she said, answering her own question as she pushed away her plate. She wasn't hungry anymore.

"I don't get it," YoYo said, putting down her toast. "What does 'retired' mean?"

Aunt Baby gave Janey a dirty look, then put her big square hand on YoYo's small jammy one. "It's nothing for a little girl to have to worry about," she said, looking only at YoYo—but speaking to Janey. "I just don't see how your grandfather can stop working now that the family's gotten so big."

"It was bigger before," Janey said stonily.

"Oh, Janey—you know what I mean," Aunt Baby said. "Two more mouths to feed."

"We don't eat very much," YoYo said in her tiniest voice. She tried to shield the mound of jam on her toast from Aunt Baby's view.

"That's not what she meant, YoYo," Janey said. "It's just an expression. But you mean the problem is all the clothes you guys will have to buy for us, and the shoes and stuff, don't you?" she asked her great-aunt.

Poppy had always complained jokingly about the cost of the girls' shoes—even as he was buying them extra pairs, "just because."

"Your Poppy knows what little girls love," Mommy had always said, rolling her eyes.

Aunt Baby nodded reluctantly. "That, and the special lessons, and sports equipment, and so on. Not to mention what we'll have to spend on tuition, if it turns out you girls need to go to private schools for some reason. And counseling, if that Ramiro woman was right. Not that we could even consider an expense like that, now. Maybe after we get some kind of settlement—from that *woman*."

YoYo jumped to her feet. "My Poppy had lots of money in the bank," she said, face blazing with indignation. "Use that up, if you think we eat so much!" She began to run from the kitchen, then doubled back, picked up her soggy toast, and fled. Aunt Baby groaned aloud and started after her.

"No, wait," Janey said, and to her surprise, Aunt Baby hesitated at the door. "*Didn't* Mommy and Poppy have any money in the bank?" she asked the woman gently.

"Of course they did," Aunt Baby said, sitting down with a thud. "Oh," she said to herself, "this didn't go at all the way I planned. I was only wanting to explain about the lawsuit."

"But what happened to Mommy and Poppy's money?" Janey said, sticking to the point.

"There was the expense of the memorial service, of course, and the cemetery plot. And then a lot of it is going to pay debts," Aunt Baby said, sighing. "Mastercard and so on. The house was your parents' main asset, but that's just now gone on the market. And it doesn't look as though we'll get quite as much for it as we thought we would. Of course, your father did have an insurance policy," she added, as if trying to think of something positive she could say about the situation.

"That's good, isn't it?" Janey asked loyally, though she felt like bursting into tears, for some reason.

She was experiencing the odd sensation of not quite knowing what to make of all the various things she was feeling: embarrassment that her parents hadn't left more money in the bank; shame at even thinking such a thing; regret that Grandpa was going to have to sell about a million toilets and bathtubs just to put fried eggs and jam into their stomachs; and fury with Aunt Baby for bringing the whole subject up in the first place.

And that was only for starters.

"Sure it is, honey," Aunt Baby said, looking as though she wasn't quite certain how the conversation had gotten away from her to this extent. "It's just that the money's not going to go as far as we might have hoped, that's all."

"So basically, you lied," Janey stated. Her voice sounded funny.

"*What?*"

"You lied," Janey repeated. "You know, when you

said that suing that drunk driver who killed Mommy and Poppy wasn't about the money."

"I—I—"

"You lied," Janey said for the third time. "Admit it!" Her voice was high now, and shaking. In fact, Janey noticed, surprised, her hands were shaking, too.

"I'll admit no such thing, young lady," Aunt Baby said, getting clumsily to her feet.

"Well, if this isn't about the money, then why don't you sue that woman for something else?" Janey asked. "Sue her for—oh, for chocolate chip cookies, why don't you? YoYo would love that. And so would you!" Janey heard herself starting to giggle.

The sound seemed to be coming from far away.

The look on Aunt Baby's face brought it nearer, however, and then Janey was absolutely shaking with laughter.

"Janey, I think you must have just lost your mind completely," Aunt Baby finally managed to say. "I never heard of such a thing."

Really, this was probably as close to being speechless as Aunt Baby would ever get. At that thought, Janey couldn't help it—she started to laugh even harder. And she could not stop.

It was a spooky sound that shocked even her.

"That does it! I'm calling Nancy," Aunt Baby said, appalled. "And then I'm calling your grandfather, too. Why should I have to handle this all alone?"

"You shouldn't! You shouldn't! You shouldn't!"

"You go lie down, Janey Bishop. Right this very minute!"

CHAPTER NINE

Dr. Vilner

Janey thought for a moment about the woman—Dr. Vilner—who was standing next to her bed; this was the "Nancy" her great-aunt had threatened her with. Nancy Vilner was an old college friend of Aunt Baby's who practiced medicine in Los Angeles, but lived nearby.

Janey *didn't* feel threatened by Dr. Vilner, though, and she was trying to figure out why. Maybe it was because she, Janey, was exhausted from totally losing it the way she had. Perhaps all feeling was finally gone.

Or maybe, Janey thought, it was because Dr. Vilner reminded her of a crazy mixture of the hospital's ever-calm Ms. Ramiro, who had tried so hard to talk to her in Phoenix; of her favorite children's librarian in Flagstaff, who loved kids' books so much that she sometimes cried with laughter when she was reading a funny one aloud; and of Dr. Seuss's Grinch.

Dr. Vilner wasn't Grinch-like because of her coloring, of course, or because she was nasty or reptilian in any way. But she did *look* a little like the Grinch: tall and gangly, with a wide, nearly lipless mouth—although Dr. Vilner's turned up at the corners in what seemed to be a permanent wry smile—and lots of wrinkles around her bright black eyes. Her grizzled hair looked as though it had been chopped off at shoulder length by a weed-whacker.

Janey liked her at once. "I'm sorry Aunt Baby made you come over," she said, pulling the brown-and-cream plaid sofa-bed blanket up under her still-unbandaged chin. "You didn't need to. I may not look like it, but I'm fine. Aunt Baby and I just had a fight, that's all. I guess she's not very used to fighting."

Dr. Vilner laughed, putting away the little flashlight with which she had just checked Janey's pupils. "You mean she's not used to anyone fighting *back*."

"Well, anyway, I'm sorry."

Sorry, sorry, sorry.

Janey let her gaze wander to the pulled shades at the windows—yanked down by a trembling Aunt

Baby as if that might trick Janey into thinking it was time to go to sleep! — and to the clothes spilling out of her duffel bag.

Two days earlier, she had still been in the hospital. Janey almost missed the old place. Some tapioca pudding would taste good right about now.

"That's okay," Dr. Vilner said, shrugging. "I had the day off, and I was going to try to find an excuse to drop in later anyway, to meet you and YoYo."

"You were? How come?"

Dr. Vilner looked surprised. "Because your great-aunt is one of my best friends, and she's worried sick about you two, of course," she said. She settled back into her chair and stretched out her long, thin legs, crossing them at the ankles.

Janey was too exhausted to reply to this, although to her, Aunt Baby seemed peeved, put out, irked at the turn her life had taken. Not worried.

"She doesn't act worried," Janey finally replied, daring to voice the thought. She had run out of things to stare at, so she shut her eyes tight as if that might give her courage. Her sides still ached from laughing so hard. "Aunt Baby acts like we're these two little pains in the neck who came along and ruined her plans. And Grandpa's plans," she added, thinking of her poor grandfather—who would still be slaving away when he was a hundred, probably. Thanks to her and YoYo.

She held her breath. Where was she getting the nerve to say stuff like this? And Dr. Vilner hadn't even given her the calming-down pill yet that Aunt Baby had also threatened her with!

Dr. Vilner didn't seem too shocked at what Janey was saying, however. In fact, she let out a bark of laughter. "Well, I'm sure you can be a pain in the neck when you put your mind to it," she finally said. "And YoYo, too."

Janey opened her eyes a fraction of an inch and smiled a little. "I guess," she admitted. "Only we haven't even been the teensiest bit bad, not so far," she said in a rush. "We haven't had a chance to, yet! But Aunt Baby's so freaked-out now. What's going to happen when she actually has to fix us supper each night and find clean clothes that YoYo will consent to wear every morning? What's she going to do when one of us does something really terrible?"

"Got anything special planned?" Dr. Vilner asked, looking curious.

"No."

"Well, I must say I see what you mean," Dr. Vilner

said slowly, leaning back in Grandpa's cracked leather swivel chair and clasping her hands over her concave stomach.

"Aunt Baby's just not—not equipped for all this," Janey said, trying to explain further.

To her annoyance, Dr. Vilner laughed. "I'll say!"

"It's not funny," Janey said, sitting up in bed. "How would you feel if you were a kid, and all of a sudden you had Aunt Baby taking care of *you?*"

"Absolutely terrified," Dr. Vilner said flatly. "But," she said, holding up her index finger, "I'd also know she would do one heck of a good job, or die trying."

Janey shrank back onto her pillow at those last words.

Dr. Vilner smacked her forehead with the palm of her hand. "Oh, Janey, I'm sorry I put it like that. What a dope I am. Forgive me?"

Janey had never heard a doctor talk like this before. Her Flagstaff doctor, Dr. Ruhoffer, didn't even seem to like kids very much—except for YoYo, who called him Dr. Roo. Also, Dr. Ruhoffer was almost deaf. You had to shout, "I have a sore throat!" at him from about two inches away just so he could hear you. And of course your throat felt even worse after that.

"Are you scared that your Aunt Baby's going to die, Janey?" Dr. Vilner asked.

Janey's heart thudded once. "Well, what if she does die? And what if Grandpa dies, too?" she asked, pulling the blanket up even tighter. "YoYo and I are running out of people," she said, trying for a joke— even a lame one.

Dr. Vilner sighed. "Yeah," she said, "I guess you are, honey. But I think Irene and your Grandpa have quite a few good years left. Enough to get you and YoYo up and running, anyway."

"You do? Really?"

Dr. Vilner nodded. "And I'm speaking as an extremely competent doctor, don't forget," she said, grinning at her own words.

Janey's grip on the blanket eased a little.

"How are you feeling, otherwise?" Dr. Vilner asked. "Apart from cracking up just the teensiest little bit, I mean."

"I'm okay," Janey replied, touching her face. And then, feeling that something more was expected, she said, "My head doesn't hurt as much as it did."

Sometimes I have to remind myself to breathe, though, she added silently. She knew how bizarre the words would sound if she said them aloud.

But really, why *should* she be breathing? Why did she survive the car accident when Mommy and Poppy had been killed?

It didn't make any sense.

"Well, I'm not a pediatrician, but I am a doctor, and your Aunt Baby filled me in a little about your medical condition," Dr. Vilner said. "I don't think it would hurt you at all to take a few extra naps for a couple of days. And when you wake up, go out in the backyard and goof around. Have some fun!"

Janey nodded, as if this was the sort of medical advice she was used to getting.

But what was she supposed to do in Grandpa's backyard? Play tag with herself?

"I'm going to leave this little pill for you," Dr. Vilner continued, placing a tablet on top of Grandpa's bookcase, where Janey could reach it but YoYo couldn't. "It'll put you right to sleep, if that's what you think you need right now. But it's up to you whether or not to take it. Let's see," she asked herself, "what else did I want to tell you?" She twiddled her fingers on her chin as if that might help her think.

Pure Grinch, Janey thought, delighted. "How come you call Aunt Baby 'Reeny' but she calls you 'Dr. Vilner'?" she asked.

"She calls me 'Doctor' when she's sick or scared," Dr. Vilner said, smiling again, "and she calls me 'Nancy' whenever my office sends her a bill. That's when she likes to remind me that we're old friends." Janey smiled, too, being a little familiar now with Aunt Baby's anxious attitude regarding money, and Dr. Vilner gave a comic shrug and stood up to go. "Anything you want me to tell your Aunt Baby?" she asked Janey.

"Tell her it's all right if I laugh," Janey said.

"Maybe it's about time you cried, did you ever think of that?" Dr. Vilner asked, tilting her head.

But she just couldn't, Janey wanted to say. If she started crying, she might never be able to stop. And then who would take care of YoYo?

She had made a promise, out there in the desert.

Instead, she said, "I guess I just don't feel like it. Yet," she added, hoping that might be an encouraging enough response to get Dr. Vilner off her back.

Dr. Vilner waited a moment, but Janey didn't say anything more. "Well, I know you'll be going over to UCLA in a few weeks to see that specialist the doctors in Arizona recommended. But in the meantime, I'm going to give your Aunt Baby a list of good pediatricians in the area," she said. "And I'll try to get her to find you girls a good counselor, too, though she's going to drag her heels on that one."

"How come?" Janey asked, although the thought of jabbering on and on about how bad she was feeling—the way Ms. Ramiro had seemed to want her to do—was not at all appealing.

"She says it's the money," Dr. Vilner said. "But that's not it. The money angle could be worked out. No, she's just old-fashioned. And I think her feelings on the subject are just all tied in to how angry she is with the woman who caused your accident."

"Huh."

"But anyone in your situation should have someone special to talk to," Dr. Vilner continued. "Speaking of which, here's my pager number," she added, stooping down to write a number on a scrap of paper, which she folded and handed to Janey. "You can make do with me, if you want, until someone better comes along. All you have to do is call this number and then punch in your own phone number, and I'll call you back as soon as I can. Now, I don't give this out to just anyone, you know," she said teasingly. "You're one of a select few."

"Oh," Janey said, pleased.

"It doesn't have to be an emergency, mind," the

doctor said. "Call if you just want to have a word in private. Or if you start laughing like a hyena again. And be *sure* to call if your Aunt Baby looks like she's about to drop dead, of course. I want to be the first to know. Or among the first."

Janey stared at her, not quite able to believe her ears. But then she couldn't help it, she did start laughing again—only now it wasn't the out-of-control giggle that had scared Aunt Baby so much. This was a real belly laugh. The first in a long time.

Dr. Vilner was just too funny!

Talking with her really made Janey miss being with Ramona and Stacy.

Aunt Baby must be okay, deep down inside, Janey thought—if she was friends with someone like Dr. Vilner.

CHAPTER TEN

The Trouble With YoYo

Janey didn't take the pill Dr. Vilner had left, but she slept anyway, enjoying a long, untroubled nap. She hadn't rolled over even once, from what she could tell when she awakened.

She looked at the clock on Grandpa's desk: three P.M. It was the middle of the afternoon already. Her mother would have told her she'd have trouble falling asleep that night, but Janey didn't think she would; she felt as though she could sleep for a week and still not feel groggy. And that was weird, because she'd slept so much in the hospital.

Her healing face felt tight and hot. It itched a little bit, too, but she tried not to scratch it. Maybe this was like chicken pox, Janey thought, where you could get scars if you scratched at the wrong time. She applied some more of the cream the hospital had sent home with her, as she looked at her face in the bathroom mirror.

It wasn't as if she thought they'd be able to make her beautiful at UCLA, she told herself. She'd never been beautiful, although Poppy always said he thought she was pretty.

Norrie Bishop had been the real beauty in the family. She'd had short hair, just a cap of butterscotch-colored curls, green eyes, and a tawny complexion. Her arms were sprinkled with freckles that Janey used to love to count, or pretend to count. Really, she just loved touching her mother, and her mother loved being touched. She was like a cat.

Poppy had shiny black hair that wouldn't lie flat no matter how much he tried to make it, dark brown eyes that could flash with humor or shine with tenderness, and black lashes and brows that Janey wished she had inherited. She had her dad's smile, though—crooked, and she had a dimple in her left cheek when she smiled, like him.

The smile dimple was still there, underneath each day's layers of gauze bandages, plastic wrap, and Silvadene; Janey had checked. It wasn't making many appearances these days, however.

YoYo looked a lot like Poppy, Janey mused, except

Poppy had been thin, and YoYo was still plump. But she had Poppy's coloring; she was "brown as a berry," Mommy always said—although that saying made no sense at all to Janey.

What berries were brown?

YoYo had the same color hair as Poppy, too. She had tried to cut it herself, just before Easter, and it was still growing out.

But the reporters had seemed to love her ragamuffin look.

YoYo. The trouble with YoYo was that Aunt Baby was spoiling her silly, Janey thought, her mood changing. Throwing the tantrum at McDonald's the way she had, and drinking all the soda she wanted, and calling herself miracle child, and twirling around for the reporters. Showing off. She was turning into a little monster.

Janey remembered again the promise she'd made, moments after the accident: *Don't worry, YoYo—I'll take care of you.*

Anxiety settled over Janey like a too-heavy quilt. How was she supposed to take care of a five-year-old, especially with Aunt Baby dressing her up like a doll and Grandpa saying "Whatever your little heart desires!" whenever YoYo asked for something?

The trouble with YoYo was that she *liked* being spoiled.

Well, Janey asked herself, trying to be fair, what kid wouldn't?

But Mommy and Poppy had hated show-offs, and YoYo was *their* little girl, not Aunt Baby's and Grandpa's.

It was up to her, Janey, to make sure YoYo turned out right, Janey thought fiercely—no matter how hard a job it was. She could do at least that much for her little sister.

And for Mommy and Poppy.

Janey emerged from Grandpa's study to find YoYo sprawled on the sofa in the living room with Birdy on her lap, watching cartoons. She was wearing a white T-shirt and socks, but also her old red shorts, which was a good sign, Janey thought. Maybe her miracle-child days were coming to an end.

Aunt Baby seemed too busy and tired to care much about that, now that they'd left Arizona. After all, no one here—apart from a couple of neighbors, Janey guessed—even knew anything about the accident, so what point would there be in making YoYo keep on dressing the part of miracle child?

A bowl of dry Raisin Bran sat perched in YoYo's lap, and she was dipping into it from time to time with a sticky hand and then cramming the cereal into her mouth without once looking away from the TV screen. Cereal lay sprinkled around her; she could have fed a small flock of birds with what was on the sofa and floor.

YoYo's other hand twirled a hunk of her hair.

"Where's Aunt Baby?" Janey asked.

"Taking a nap," YoYo said, not taking her eyes off the flickering images on the screen. "She told me not to move unless I had to go potty."

Janey considered her options. If she grabbed the remote and turned off the TV, YoYo would go ape and Aunt Baby would wake up. If she ignored her sister, YoYo wouldn't even notice; it was as though she were mesmerized by the show she was watching. If she scolded YoYo about spilling cereal all over the place, the little girl would probably throw the rest of the Raisin Bran into the air, she'd been acting so weird lately.

And so Janey sat down next to her. "Can I have a bite?" she asked, pointing to the cereal bowl.

"Yeah, but don't eat all the raisins," YoYo said, still watching the screen.

Janey sighed as she dipped her hand into the bowl. "Mommy doesn't like it when you say 'yeah,'" she reminded her sister. "She says you should say 'yes.'"

"So?"

Janey's hand froze midway to her mouth. *So?* She hadn't expected that one. "Well," she said mildly, "I was just reminding you of what Mommy likes. Liked."

Nothing.

"Can't you at least say thanks?" Janey said, feeling a little foolish.

"No, I can't," YoYo said sullenly, and she hugged the cereal bowl to her chest. "Get your own snack," she said, finally looking Janey in the eye.

"But there's enough here for—"

"Get your own," YoYo interrupted coldly, and she turned back to the TV. "Hamburger face," she added, seemingly to no one in particular.

Janey felt herself blush.

This was going to be harder than she'd thought.

CHAPTER ELEVEN

Boris Morris

"So, what happened to *you*?" Boris Morris said a week later, giving Janey the once-over.

Janey blushed, which of course only made her face look worse under its patchwork of bandages, and she kicked her heel moodily at Grandpa's neighbors' redwood picnic table bench. "I was in an accident," she replied.

Some swell idea *this* was.

But YoYo was playing with Monica, the little girl down the street who was reputed to have more than forty Barbies, and Aunt Baby had announced at breakfast that Janey had an invitation, too. "He's a nice boy," Aunt Baby said, sounding a little doubtful, "but he's *Russian*. They adopted him. He's almost eleven now, I think. Quiet. Keeps to himself. A loner, I guess you'd say."

Oh, great, Janey thought moodily. They'd fixed up a play date for her—her, a twelve-year-old!—with someone who fit every description she'd ever heard of a serial killer. "I'd rather stay here," she told Aunt Baby. "I'm right at the exciting part of my book."

"You're going over to the Morrises to play," Aunt Baby had stated flatly. "I have a hair appointment, and I wouldn't miss it for the world."

"But what happened, exactly?" Boris repeated, tilting his head in inquiry.

Janey shot him a dirty look.

He was a short little kid, and skinny and pale. He didn't look like a Californian, in Janey's opinion, although he did not sound foreign. His light brown hair was buzz cut, for summer, she guessed, and his scalp showed pink through the bristles. His eyes were almost golden, and his lashes were so blond that they were practically invisible.

"I was in a *car* accident," Janey told him, adding the word reluctantly. She kicked the bench again. "You shouldn't make comments about the way a person looks," she added, hating him. "We don't do that in America." She sneaked another look at him to see how this remark had gone down.

Good! Now *he* was blushing.

"I'm just as much an American as you," he said. "And I'm probably a lot smarter, too."

"Oh, I doubt that," Janey said, feeling mean. "I'm more than a year older than you. And anyway, how come your name is Boris, if you're such an American? That's a vampire's name. Or a spy's. *Boris Morris*," she said, sounding both spooky and sarcastic.

Boris shrugged, as if nothing she said could hurt him. But his face turned red so fast that it was as if he were a TV set and someone had suddenly fiddled with his color control.

Janey's heart beat faster, seeing his anger, but she didn't apologize. This was kind of fun, she thought, feeling only a little bit guilty. Maybe it was "the new her," as one of Ramona's fashion magazines might have put it. She would develop a nasty personality to go along with her new face.

No more too-nice, wishy-washy Janey! If only Stacy and Ramona were here. How "comfy" was she to be with now?

"Vampire," she repeated for good measure.

Boris sat on the picnic table, fuming. "What's the square root of thirty-six?" he asked suddenly.

The—*huh*? "Who cares?" Janey said, since she didn't have the slightest idea what the correct answer was.

After all, it was summer. Who thought about math during the summer?

"Lots of people care," he said, sneering. "You just don't know, that's all. But I do. I can do almost any equation in my head."

"Big deal," Janey told him. "I can do the same thing with a calculator."

But she *was* impressed.

Boris looked at his watch, then seemed to make the decision to calm down and try to talk nicely to Janey. "Was your little sister hurt, too? In the accident?" he asked, jumping down from the table and sitting down cross-legged on the grass.

"No. 'She escaped without a scratch,'" Janey said, quoting from a newspaper article Aunt Baby had saved.

Boris wasn't the only one who could memorize stuff!

"It was a miracle, really," Janey added.

"There's no such thing as miracles," Boris said, smiling a little to himself and shaking his head, as if pitying Janey's primitive superstitious beliefs.

Janey shrugged, pretending to be bored. "I'm just telling you what the newspapers said."

Boris snorted. "The newspapers print horoscopes. Do you believe in them, too?"

Horoscopes! What would he come up with next?

Ramona definitely believed in horoscopes, Janey remembered, although Stacy had been skeptical of them. "My cat was born in April, too," she'd scoffed once. "Does that mean that since we're both Aries, Domino should take care not to quarrel with family members today? And that she should avoid self-deception?"

Ramona had laughed out loud in triumph. "Well, how come you know your sign, if you don't believe in horoscopes so much?" she asked—not unreasonably, Janey had thought at the time. "And you obviously read yours today!"

Janey sometimes read hers, too.

Boris threw his hands up in a shrug that was intended to signify hopelessness. "This girl doesn't even know *what* she believes," he said to no one in particular.

"I do too know what I believe," Janey said, her voice practically a snarl. "And no, I do *not* believe in horoscopes."

"What sign are you?" Boris asked her—quick as a wink, as Poppy sometimes put it.

"Cancer," Janey replied, before she could stop herself.

Cancer, surely the least wonderful sounding of all the signs.

"Hah," Boris said, as if he had just solved a not-too-difficult equation.

"Shut up," Janey told him. "At least I'm not a Russian Communist."

"Dummy," he said. "It's the *Soviets* who were the Communists. At least some of them. But then the Soviet Union got changed back to Russia. Everybody knows that! It was in the newspaper," he added, mocking her.

"So what were you?" Janey asked him. "Soviet or Russian?"

Boris gave a smaller shrug this time. "I was nobody. I was just an orphan," he said, seeming to find the whole subject boring, now. "My California mom and dad came over to Russia and adopted me. They picked me out from all the rest," he said, as if he too were quoting someone. He blinked once, as though he were still amazed at having been so chosen.

"How old were you?"

"Four. Not that it's any of your business," Boris said, clasping his thin white arms around his knees as if he were somehow under attack. "My parents told me that my new name was going to be Stevie, but I told the translator that I wanted to stick with Boris. Because that's the name my Russian mom gave me."

"Well, now you know how I feel," Janey said, thinking that this would enable her to point out that it wasn't any of *his* business about the car accident.

"Why?" he asked, sneering at her once more. "Are you an orphan, too?"

"Yeah, I am."

It just slipped out.

But for the first time, Janey almost believed it.

"I really didn't know your parents were killed," Boris said to her about fifteen minutes later, after she'd told him her story, or at least what she remembered of it. "I'm sorry. My mom and dad didn't tell me. Were you guys coming here on vacation?"

"Sort of," Janey said.

"It can be really fun here—in Southern California, I mean," Boris said, babbling a little in his embarrassment. "You know, you can to go to Disneyland . . . and Universal Studios and the beach . . . and stuff. Magic Mountain, too."

"Have you been to all those places?" Janey asked, feeling a little envious.

"Sure," he said. "I like the beach best. Except I have to be careful not to get sunburned. What do you have back where you come from?"

Janey thought for a moment. "We're pretty near the Grand Canyon," she said. "That's the most famous thing about Flagstaff."

"That's *cool*," he admitted. "We went there two summers ago. We rode on mules and everything."

"Really? Cool," Janey echoed. She tried to picture Boris bouncing down the trail from Bright Angel Lodge, perhaps doing advanced math problems in his head to pass the time, but she couldn't. "Did your family drive through Flagstaff?" she asked.

Boris nodded.

"That's where we used to live," Janey said softly.

Boris had actually come through her hometown with his family, she thought, amazed. The Morrises' car might have passed Poppy's poor doomed Toyota on the street, or she and her friends might have walked by them—just another tourist family—as they strolled along lower Leroux or busy Santa Fe Avenue.

It was weird, almost scary, to think of the two worlds colliding this way: her old Flagstaff life, and her new Glendale life.

Her past, and her future.

Ramona probably would have laughed at that goofy sight-seeing Boris—even before hearing his name.

Janey kind of liked him, though. She couldn't say why.

But at least she didn't feel so totally alone anymore.

CHAPTER TWELVE

The Really Important Things About Flagstaff

"I've got a fun idea," Janey said to YoYo the next morning during breakfast, after Aunt Baby had gone into the garage to start a load of wash. "Let's play school."

The thing was, she figured, YoYo must simply have forgotten the sort of stuff Mommy and Poppy didn't like her to do. She obviously didn't remember the rules about drinking juice, not soda, and not eating in the living room except when they were having a party, and not saying "Yeah."

Well, a little forgetting was natural enough, Janey thought, trying to be generous. YoYo had always needed reminding about things, so this plan was perfect! Her little sister loved playing school. She couldn't wait to go to kindergarten.

YoYo looked tempted by Janey's suggestion, but

she said, "I can't. I'm going over to Monica's house to play dolls."

"Not until later this afternoon," Janey said. Boris was coming over then; he was teaching her how to play his newest handheld video game. It had tilt technology, he boasted—whatever that was.

She tried not to think of Stacy and Ramona, back in Flagstaff. Janey had probably disappeared from their thoughts as surely as if she'd never even existed. They were probably sitting on the floor in Stacy's room right this very moment, planning what to do that hot August day.

If they thought of her at all, it was probably to remember how mean she'd been to them when she was in the hospital. *Meeny.*

"But I want to play with Monica now," YoYo said, lower lip trembling.

"Come on, YoYo—I'll let you use my best colored markers if we play school." This was a real enticement, because YoYo loved anything that had to do with art, and Janey had been guarding her new art supplies ferociously.

Aunt Baby reappeared at the kitchen door, popping into the room like a stout little cuckoo clock figure. "Finish your breakfast, girls. Want to make some cookies with me when you're done?" she asked, obviously trying to come up with something that would occupy them for the entire morning.

"We can't," Janey said firmly. "We're just about to play school. Maybe later, though. *Colored markers*," she whispered to YoYo, reminding her of the promise she'd made.

"Why don't *you* make the cookies," YoYo suggested to Aunt Baby over her shoulder after she and Janey had cleared the table and were leaving the room. "We'll eat them!"

"Okay," Janey said, settling down with her sister on a shady patch of lawn in the backyard. A hummingbird buzzed low over her head, intent on reaching a nearby clump of flowers, and YoYo ducked involuntarily.

"Was that a bumblebee?" the little girl asked, cringing. YoYo was scared of all bees and spiders and most insects—now more than ever. She looked as though she was on the brink of changing her mind about how to spend the morning.

"It was just a little bird," Janey reassured her. "You're perfectly safe."

Safe, she thought, a sudden hollow feeling in her

chest. People were just plain dumb if they thought they were ever really safe.

Because things could change in a second.

Still, she wanted YoYo to feel safe.

"Let's color," YoYo said, already having forgotten the hummingbird incident. She started yanking the tops off Janey's newest markers and tossing them onto the grass as she inspected each color so closely that she ended up with dabs of purple, orange, and green on her nose.

Janey gritted her teeth but didn't scold. She wanted YoYo right here, where she could keep an eye on her. "Want me to show you how to print your name?" she asked.

"I already know," YoYo bragged. She bent low over her pad and printed TOTO, her tongue poking out with the effort.

So she was still having trouble with her Ys. Wait until she tried to spell *Eucalyptus*, Janey thought grimly.

"There," YoYo said proudly.

"Okay," Janey said. "Now let's draw our old house in Flagstaff." She wasn't quite sure she could do this herself, but it was worth a try. Anything to keep YoYo from forgetting.

"That's easy," YoYo said, reaching for a red marker.

Their old house had been white, but Janey kept her mouth shut. She selected a brown marker, though, to outline a pure white house.

"That's a yucky color," YoYo told her, drawing a huge front door with a big doorknob right in the middle of it.

"I like it," Janey said, drawing a steeply pitched roof. There, she thought. But they'd had three trees in front, hadn't they? Two tall triangular ones that framed the big front window, and an even taller one between the front porch and the alley? But what kind of trees were they? Some kind of evergreen.

"I'm putting in cats," YoYo informed her.

"We didn't have any cats. Poppy was allergic to them, remember?"

"We had lots of cats," YoYo said firmly. She started in on their whiskers.

Lots of cats. Okay, Janey told herself. That wasn't so bad—not as long as her sister remembered the really important things about Flagstaff. "Why don't you draw Mommy and Poppy?" she suggested.

"I'm too busy," YoYo said, coloring the doorknob purple.

"Come on," Janey coaxed. "I'll let you wear my old hospital bracelet if you do." YoYo had been admitted to Children's Hospital for observation only, and her treasured plastic ID bracelet had been accidentally discarded later by motel housekeeping—much to her sorrow. She was jealous that Janey had been able to hang on to hers.

"Really?" YoYo said, looking up from under her tangled bangs. "For how long?"

"All day."

"And all night?" YoYo asked, wheedling.

"Sure," Janey said. What did she care? She wasn't wearing it anymore. She didn't even know why she'd kept it.

"Okay," YoYo said, bending over her pad of newsprint once more. "Here's Mommy." She drew a stick figure woman wearing a long skirt, then selected a black marker and started drawing loopy curls that cascaded down way past the figure's shoulders. She hummed a little as she worked.

Janey toyed with the brown marker. "Mommy usually wore shorts in the summer," she finally reminded her sister. "Even on hikes."

"Well, this mom wears beautiful dresses—all the time," YoYo said, drawing a few more ringlets. She cocked her head, admiring her efforts.

This mom? "You're supposed to be drawing *our* mom," Janey reminded her. "That was the deal, YoYo."

"This *is* our mom."

"No, it's not. Our mom didn't have long curly black hair." *You dummy*, she felt like adding, but she didn't. "Look, YoYo—our mom's hair was more of a goldy brown, remember? Like this color," Janey said, exchanging her marker for a lighter one. "And her hair was real short."

"I wanna draw her like this," YoYo said, not looking at her sister.

"Then draw Poppy instead, okay?" Janey said. She could feel her heart beating in her throat, she was so upset by what was happening. Had YoYo really forgotten what their mother looked like?

YoYo shrugged. "Okay, but stop yelling at me," she warned.

"I will. But remember, Poppy had black hair."

YoYo sighed and started drawing on a new piece of paper, hiding her picture from Janey's view with the crook of her arm as she worked. "Why don't you go get the bracelet for me? I'm almost done," she finally said.

"I want to see the picture first," Janey told her sternly.

Silent, YoYo straightened up and slowly pulled her arm away from the paper. A tall stick figure stretched from the top to the bottom of the page. The figure was wearing huge red shoes, and a shock of black zigzaggy lines—a fairly accurate depiction of Poppy's hair, Janey had to admit—crowned the round head. A big hat perched atop the figure's hair.

"He's skinny, see?" YoYo said, pointing. "And those are his favorite red sneakers. I wore 'em once."

"That is correct," Janey told her, teacherlike.

Her heart seemed to twist in her chest, though, when she remembered those shoes. "My walloping clodhoppers," Poppy called them. And she remembered the evening a dripping wet and totally bare YoYo shuffled into the living room fresh from her bath, wearing them on her tiny feet.

It looked more as if the big red sneakers were wearing *her*.

Janey and her mom and dad had laughed until they cried, clutching one another for support.

"But what's with the hat?" Janey asked.

"You know," YoYo said. "It's like in that picture."

"What picture?"

"The one on Grandpa's desk," YoYo said impatiently.

Janey bit her lips together with matching impatience. Yes, there was a photograph of Poppy and Mommy on Grandpa's desk, and *yes*, Poppy was wearing a hat in the picture, but it was one of the few times Janey could ever remember him wearing one.

Poppy said hats made his hair look even funnier than usual.

Did this mean that YoYo would always think of miniature faces grinning out of old photographs when she tried to remember what their parents looked like? What about the unphotographed moments that were much truer: Mommy singing a silly made-up lullaby in the dark while she stroked your hair, or Poppy accidentally flipping a pancake onto the floor on Sunday morning?

And YoYo *eating* it?

Janey swallowed hard as she realized that while she could recall these things, and a hundred others, even *she* could no longer picture her parents' faces with any clarity. Their smells, yes. The lemon fragrance of Mommy's light perfume lingered somewhere in Janey's memory, as did the woodsy scent of Poppy's shaving soap.

But their faces—their faces seemed to be floating away from her.

"Poppy always wore a hat," YoYo said, sounding a little uncertain.

"Yeah, you're right. He did," Janey quickly agreed.

It was only a little fib, after all.

CHAPTER THIRTEEN

Out of the Habit

"I want to go with Grandpa, too," YoYo shrieked the following Saturday morning, pounding her fists so hard on the sofa cushions that a couple of little white feathers popped out and swirled crazily in the air. Tears spurted from YoYo's eyes and coursed down her round cheeks, leaving shiny stripes behind them.

Janey watched her from the hallway door. *Uh-oh, here come the waterworks*, Poppy would have said, rolling his eyes.

"I never get to do anything around here!" YoYo sobbed, burying her head in her hands.

Maybe YoYo was going to grow up to be an actress, Janey thought gloomily. That might be what happened when you moved to California.

Aunt Baby stopped wringing her hands and crouched down next to the little girl. "Sweetheart, you get to come with *me*," she said, trying to make it sound like fun. "We're going to get the car washed. And then visit a friend of mine. And—and then," she added, obviously making it up on the spot, "we'll go out for ice cream!"

"How many scoops?" YoYo asked in a hiccupy voice, not raising her head.

"Um, two?" Aunt Baby said, as if trying to come up with the correct answer.

A double-decker, Janey thought, outraged. *Just for having another temper tantrum!*

"Ready to go, darlin'?" Grandpa whispered behind her.

"Sure. I guess," Janey whispered back, and they sneaked out the kitchen door.

"Buckle up," Grandpa reminded her, and then he was silent.

That was the good thing about running errands with Grandpa, Janey mused—he didn't jabber on and on about nothing. Unlike Aunt Baby, who seemed to view any silent moment as a catastrophe during which anything could happen. What was she so afraid of?

And what was up with YoYo and all those tears?

Mommy and Poppy had only been gone—*gone*, everyone said, as though Janey's parents had simply taken off on an extended vacation—for a month, it was true. But still, shouldn't YoYo be pulling herself together a little better by now?

After all, YoYo had Monica, her friend with all the dolls.

She had new toys galore.

Thanks to Aunt Baby, YoYo was even accumulating brand-new clothes for kindergarten, although class wouldn't start for another month. To judge by the outfits Aunt Baby had selected, YoYo's kindergarten class was going to be held on some tropical island. "That doesn't really look very practical for fall," Janey said once, feeling like a fuddy-duddy as she eyed a pink shorts set with matching rickrack-trimmed socks.

"September is just about our hottest month here in Southern California," Aunt Baby replied, refolding the small pink T-shirt. "It's not like in Flagstaff, Janey. We can't have poor little YoYo sweltering in class."

YoYo had her familiar old videos from Leroux Street; she had Aunt Baby to cuddle her; she had Grandpa to read her bedtime stories in his rumbly voice.

And she had her, Janey.

So what was up with all the crying?

It wasn't as if YoYo were crying because she missed Mommy and Poppy, Janey thought moodily, slouched down in the front seat of the car and staring out the window as Grandpa drove down Brand Boulevard on his way to the furniture store. Oh, no. YoYo cried for a hundred other reasons: Her cocoa was too hot. She couldn't make a puzzle piece fit, no matter how hard she pounded it. She couldn't find the remote. Her socks were all slouchy down around her heels, and it just felt *terrible*.

"Want the radio on?" Grandpa asked. "I know how you kids love your music." He had a brave look on his face, as if he was facing an ordeal but was prepared to conduct himself with courage.

"No thanks," Janey said.

She couldn't relax and listen to music with Grandpa suffering beside her.

After all, she wasn't a *monster*.

But what was she, then? Janey brooded silently as the car inched its way through Glendale's Saturday morning traffic. Who else but a monster would remain dry-eyed, having gone through what *she* had?

Because although YoYo may have been crying

too much, she, Janey, hadn't cried at all.

At first, Janey remembered, she hadn't cried because it seemed as though crying would somehow make it true that Mommy and Poppy had actually died in the crash. It was as if she alone were controlling their fate.

When she'd seen her unbandaged face in the hospital mirror that terrible afternoon, she hadn't cried because—because what would have been the point? The plastic surgeon had already said the California doctors were going to do everything they could.

Besides, Janey thought, she would have felt guilty over crying about a messed-up face when her parents were dead.

Dead, not "gone."

She had almost cried after she'd driven Ramona and Stacy from her hospital room. But tears had somehow seemed to be—*not enough*, when it came to having to move away from your best friends.

She had almost cried during Mr. Chesterton's crazy press conference, true, but only because YoYo was crying. That would have been a case of contagious crying, like when you saw someone weeping on the movie screen and that made tears come to your own eyes. It wasn't the real thing.

Anyway, Janey thought fiercely, she wouldn't have given the photographers the satisfaction of getting *that* picture.

She had *definitely* almost cried the morning she'd scared Aunt Baby, when she, Janey, couldn't stop laughing. But she hadn't cried, because part of her was too busy watching—and not believing—what was happening to her.

She had almost cried when she'd told Boris about the car accident. But that would have been rude, because he hadn't even *known* Mommy and Poppy. Besides, would Boris then have expected her to cry about his dead Russian parents?

She blushed even thinking about such an awkward situation.

Really, Janey thought, sighing, she had just kind of gotten out of the habit of crying.

And hopefully, the worst was past. So, why start crying now?

Crying wouldn't solve a thing. And to cry now would somehow be a betrayal of all the sad times she'd lived through during the last few weeks, wouldn't it? Those days she *hadn't* cried?

"We're here," Grandpa announced. "Let's just hope they have something that you girls will like."

* * *

Janey followed her grandfather, who was following a saleswoman through various crowded displays of fake rooms. The saleswoman had dragged her eyes away from Janey's bandaged face without asking any questions, although clearly she'd wanted to. She was wearing so much perfume that Janey could smell it fifteen paces away.

In one of the rooms they passed, a dictionary sat open on a pretend-boy's desk as if that kid had just gotten up to go get a wholesome snack from the kitchen. His pretend-bed with its striped bedspread was neatly made, although Ramona's brother Ned—a feisty nine-year-old—seldom made *his* bed, if Janey remembered correctly. And his room smelled like a hamster cage.

A fake family room was also eerily perfect, although tucked into a bookshelf—halfway filled with books that seemed to have been chosen for the colors of their jackets—were framed "portraits" that looked as if they'd been cut from magazines. A blue-and-green plaid blanket was strewn casually across the arm of a sofa, and an empty teacup sat on a nearby coffee table. The cup was next to a book that had been splayed facedown on the wooden table.

Her old librarian in Flagstaff would have something to say about *that*, Janey thought, hiding a smile
as she read the book's title: *An Introduction to
Beekeeping.*

Yeah, right, Janey scoffed silently. This invisible
family certainly *looked* like a bunch of beekeepers!
She should have guessed.

"Here are the girls' beds," the furniture saleswoman
said, making a sweeping gesture with her manicured
hand. "We can select the mattresses later."

"It's a small room we're talking about," Grandpa
said doubtfully, peering at a huge canopied bed that
looked as if it could hold an entire fairy-tale family.
"It's tiny, really."

"Oh," the saleswoman said, sounding crestfallen.
"Well, we'll just look around," she added, deciding to
make the best of a disappointing situation. Then she
jumped a little and looked down at her waist. "I'm
being paged up front," she said, sounding apologetic.

"You go right ahead and see what they want,"
Grandpa told her. "My granddaughter and I will just
look around and make our selection."

The woman looked torn. "Don't forget, I'm
Marjorie," she finally said.

"Marjorie," Grandpa repeated. "We'll have them

page you if we find something." He and Janey watched the woman trot away, her high heels clattering on the parquet floor. "Thought she'd never leave," Grandpa whispered to Janey, surprising her.

She gave her grandfather a shy smile and looked around the display area. The saleswoman's perfume lingered in the air.

"See anything you like?" Grandpa asked.

Janey sat down and bounced experimentally on the plastic-wrapped mattress that sat atop a sample bed. "But, Grandpa," she said, refusing to fall in love with any furniture before getting out into the open what was on her mind, "there's no room for any more stuff in your study. YoYo and I are okay on the sofa bed. Really."

Grandpa sat down on a nearby bed, shaking his head. "Sofa beds are for guests, Janey. Especially when you don't want them to stay too long," he added with a sly smile. "And you and YoYo aren't guests, you're family. This is your home now, and I want it to feel like home. As much as possible, anyway," he added, seemingly to himself.

Janey stared down at her sandals.

The two of them were quiet for a minute or two, then Grandpa cleared his throat as if preparing to say something important. "We're eventually going to try to get a bigger house for the four of us, Janey, or add on to the one we have, if the lawsuit comes out the way Mr. Chesterton thinks it will. Then you and YoYo will be able to have your own rooms again, like you did when you were living in Flagstaff. Your Aunt Baby and I want things to be nice again for the two of you someday, darlin'. But in the meantime, the least we can do is to buy you kids your own beds."

"Things are okay now," Janey said, still looking at her feet.

"Things *stink* now," Grandpa corrected her. "There's no getting around it."

Janey found herself wishing she were someplace else, even though she had always liked hanging out with her grandfather during her family's annual visits to Glendale. On his days off, they would sometimes drive away alone together—to do chores, supposedly, while Mommy and Poppy were embroiled in some activity with YoYo and Aunt Baby. But Janey and Grandpa often ended up sprawled in shady Verdugo Park instead, with a bagful of hamburgers at hand and a stack of brand-new magazines to thumb through in silence with ketchupy fingers.

Once or twice, Grandpa had even brought Janey into his office with him. He always let her use the photocopy machine as much as she wanted, so she made up funny little books for Ramona and Stacy and invented games for YoYo, and printed them up.

It had been fun, she remembered. Grandpa didn't talk as much as Aunt Baby, which was a relief, and he never complained.

But now, was Grandpa saying things stunk because of the accident? Or did things stink because YoYo and Janey were hogging his study? "Well, where will you put your desk and your bookcases and file cabinets if you buy two new beds for the study?" she asked, following this last thought through to its conclusion.

"I'll put the desk in my bedroom," Grandpa said, obviously having spent some time thinking about this. "The file cabinets will go in the garage, along with the sofa bed and with any books I decide I'm going to keep."

"But where will the cars go?"

"This is California," he told her, shrugging. "They can stay in the driveway. It's not as if they'll get buried in snow."

Janey flopped back on the bed and put an arm over her eyes, shielding them against the fluorescent glare of the lights.

Grandpa's voice seemed to float down from those

very lights. "I know you miss your parents a whole heck of a lot, Janey, and I know it seems like the world's turned upside down. Everything's all wrong— for all of us. But let's just do this one thing right, okay? Let's pick out some nice furniture that will be okay for now, something that will fit into the study. Maybe it will make us both feel better."

Janey struggled to control her voice. "Okay, Grandpa," she said, sitting up and pasting a smile on her face. "Bunk beds will fit, won't they?"

CHAPTER FOURTEEN

The Mommy and Poppy Quiz

Janey sat on the old sofa bed two mornings later with a pad of paper while YoYo and Aunt Baby watched *Martha Stewart* in the next room. The new furniture—white bunk beds, a chest of drawers, and a desk—were being shipped from a factory to the furniture store's warehouse, and everything would be ready for Grandpa to pick up soon. He'd save the delivery fee that way.

But meanwhile, something had to be done about YoYo and all her forgetting, Janey thought, chewing on the end of a ballpoint pen. What would be a good way to remember all the super-important details about Mommy and Poppy?

Because, Janey now realized, it was the details that were important about a person. Not the big stuff, such as what you did for a living—Poppy taught P.E. at Sinagua High, for instance, and Mommy wanted to open a children's book store in one of those old red-brick buildings on lower Leroux someday—or how much money you made.

Janey bit her lower lip and printed a line at the top of the page: THE MOMMY AND POPPY QUIZ. She would make this fun. And YoYo was such a little know-it-all that she'd never be able to resist answering these simple questions.

1. What was Mommy's favorite thing in the world to eat for breakfast?

That was easy, Janey told herself—yogurt, granola, and fruit. Sometimes Poppy even combined them for her like an ice cream sundae in a tall fancy glass. "For you," he would say, kissing Mommy on the neck and making her blush.

2. What part of the newspaper did Poppy always read first?

This was almost too easy. The funnies, of course! Still, it was always a good idea to throw in a couple of easy questions, Janey told herself. Otherwise YoYo might get discouraged.

Poppy's favorite comic strip was *Zits*, because the main character reminded him of his students, and his second favorite was *For Better or for Worse*, and his third favorite was *Agnes*. The only one he skipped was *Mary Worth*. He said you could read that comic once a month and still keep up.

Whenever he got to *Dilbert*, he always said he was glad he didn't have to work in an office.

Janey had liked snuggling in his lap at breakfast—until she got too old, anyway—while he spent a good twenty minutes reading the funnies. He would give her little bites of toast, and she'd eat them, pretending she was a baby.

So okay, "the funnies" was the correct answer.

3. What kind of toast did Poppy like best?

Rye.

Janey wasn't sure if YoYo knew the names of different breads yet, though. Janey knew what she liked, of course. Their mother had usually made the girls eat whole-wheat bread, and YoYo wolfed it down—as long as it wasn't "too bumpy," as she put it.

The only exception Mommy made to the whole-wheat rule was in allowing the family to eat white hamburger buns, which Poppy preferred. "It's traditional," he said.

Here in Glendale, YoYo was demanding soft white bread every single day—and getting it.

Janey frowned, but she did not cross out the question.

Because "rye" was the correct answer.

4. What did we give Mommy last Mother's Day?

Janey almost laughed out loud just thinking about it. She and YoYo and Poppy had taken the Toyota to the car wash down on Milton Road one Saturday afternoon in May and brainstormed in the waiting area until they'd come up with the perfect gift.

"I wish *I* could go through the car wash," YoYo had said, watching their car get all sudsed up.

Poppy grinned. "We could send you to some fancy spa in Scottsdale," he said, naming the resort town just next to Phoenix. "They'd soap you up, and rinse you off, and shower you with perfume, and then paint your toenails shocking pink."

"I want shocking-pink toenails," YoYo said, almost beside herself with excitement. "Do it!"

"Hey, wait a minute," Janey had said. "Mommy

would *love* going to a fancy spa in Scottsdale. I heard her talking to Stacy's mom about it once. She said it sounded like her idea of heaven."

Poppy laughed. "What was the name of the spa, do you remember?"

"The Something Moonflower, or the Moonflower Something," Janey said. Going to a spa had sounded pretty cool to her, too, and at least part of the name had stuck in her head.

"Close enough," Poppy said, grinning. "We'll treat Mommy to a couple of nights in Scottsdale and to a day at the Moonflower Spa for Mother's Day. She'll absolutely adore it."

Their mother *had* loved it. She arrived home relaxed, smiling, and brimming with stories after her mini-vacation. The part that tickled Poppy most was when she told about getting something called a seaweed wrap. "That's no big deal! We can do that right here at home," he insisted, and he hustled off to the kitchen with YoYo hot on his heels.

They'd staggered back into the living room with limp lettuce leaves draped over their faces and outstretched arms.

"The Moonflower Spa" was the correct answer to question number four.

Janey wrote down the last question without even thinking.

5. Why didn't Poppy see that lady's car coming at us and swerve out of the way? And why did YoYo and I live when they died?

But she didn't know the answer to those questions, and so she got a ruler from Grandpa's desk and carefully drew a line through them.

CHAPTER FIFTEEN

Hey, Meeny!

The letter was propped up against her cereal bowl.

August 12

Hey, Meeny!

It's me, Miney.

I miss you so-o-o much, even though you did act kind of MEAN to me that time I visited you in the hospital! Not that I blame you, or anything. If you get into a car accident and suffer a concussion, my mom says, you are entitled to act weird.

FOR A WHILE.

I like YoYo, by the way. And I am so sorry about your parents.

How's life in California? I wanted to come visit you right away, but my mom and dad said that you and YoYo probably need a chance to settle in. Maybe next year, they said!

So anyway, I went camping with my dad after I visited you in the hospital, but Ramona decided not to come, even though she'd promised she would. In fact, she bailed on me—at the very last minute! And it was obviously too late to invite anyone else!!

She was probably still mad about the fight. Yes, I had a fight with THAT DARLING GIRL, which, as you know, is what my mom always calls her.

It was when we were driving home from visiting you at the hospital (or _trying_ to), as a matter of fact. I wish I could tell you what the fight was about, but I can't, because it was about NOTHING.

One minute we were eating takeout in the backseat, and the next minute we weren't speaking.

I never want to see her again.

My mom says that this is a period of change for everyone. She has been reading a lot of library books about grief lately. She is driving me crazy, always wanting to talk to me about FEELINGS.

My feelings are <u>my</u> business!!!

You are the only person I want to share them with. <u>And you aren't here</u>!!!!

Your house still has a FOR SALE sign up. If anyone buys it and moves in, I promise not to like them. I won't even talk to them.

What is your phone number in California? Are you on-line yet?? It seems like you're a million miles away.

Write soon! And don't forget me.

Love,

Stacy

P.S. If Ramona writes you, tell me what she says, okay?

CHAPTER SIXTEEN

Grandpa

Janey couldn't sleep—again.

How could Ramona and Stacy have had a fight? Didn't they know how lucky they were?

For example, they were still living in Flagstaff, in their same old houses.

They could go hang out at Wheeler Park whenever they wanted, or listen to music at Stacy's house, or admire Ramona's fluffy white comforters—from afar, of course.

They had moms and dads.

They had each other.

Just because *her* life had changed, that didn't mean their lives had to change too, did it?

In a strange way, Janey realized, she had liked to think that Ramona and Stacy were still doing all the usual stuff, even if it was without her. She'd been jealous of them, true, but knowing her friends were happy together was like—it was like knowing that the sun would come up tomorrow, as Grandpa's old saying went.

When she'd been in the hospital, Janey remembered suddenly, she hadn't been sure of that much, even. After all, the sun *hadn't* come up for Mommy and Poppy the day after the accident, had it?

And if something so bad could happen to them, it could happen to anyone.

Wasn't it possible for there to be at least one sure thing in this world?

YoYo was asleep, but she seemed to be having bad dreams; she flopped back and forth on the sofa bed, pulling the covers with her as she thrashed. "Quit it," Janey muttered once or twice, pulling them back, but she didn't want to wake her little sister.

"Hey," YoYo cried out once, sounding outraged, and Janey wondered what in the world she was dreaming about.

At least her sister wasn't having another nightmare.

Janey ran her fingertips over her bumpy face. It didn't itch at all anymore; instead, her face had become extra-sensitive. Touching it made Janey feel that she really might be alive, after all.

Inside, though, she still felt numb.

Just yesterday, Boris had said she looked better, even though she hadn't asked his opinion. Not directly. "So, what's school like, here?" she'd asked instead, watching him manipulate his video aircraft's pitch and steering with an expertise she had yet to master.

"It's okay," he said, not looking up, of course. "As long as you fit into the norm."

Janey laughed and tried not to touch the bandages that still covered the worst of her wounds. "I guess that lets me out," she said.

"Why?" he asked. "Everyone will be amazed at how tragic and brave you are when school starts, and anyway, you'll probably be pretty again by Thanksgiving. They'll like you just fine. Now me," he said, scowling ferociously at the directional pad, "I'll look like this forever. The best *I* can hope for is to be invisible. But I've just about perfected that."

She'd felt bad for him.

Next to Janey, YoYo started sucking her thumb noisily. "Quit it," Janey said again, but more gently than before. She shook YoYo's shoulder a little.

"Muh," YoYo said.

"*Muh*, yourself," Janey whispered, and she got up, taking care not to stub her toe on the sofa bed's treacherous metal frame. She didn't worry too much about making noise as she padded down the dimly lit hall to the downstairs bathroom, because Grandpa and Aunt Baby both had their bedrooms on the second floor.

A flickering light caught her attention at the end of the hall. It was coming from the living room, though everyone in the household had long since gone to bed.

Janey held her breath. A burglar? Should she scurry back to Grandpa's study and call the police? Or dash up the stairs and wake Grandpa and Aunt Baby?

No, Janey thought instantly—she could never leave YoYo alone downstairs with a burglar.

Almost as quickly, Janey realized that most likely it *wasn't* a burglar. There was no noise coming from the living room, for one thing, or very little noise, although Janey thought she heard a slight wheezing sound. And what would a wheezy burglar take from that overcrowded room, apart from the old TV and VCR? Aunt Baby's collection of giraffe figurines and stuffed animals? The long-lashed creatures were clustered in a display case near her afghan-swathed easy chair and ottoman.

YoYo was crazy about them, of course. At least the stuffed ones.

So, what was the source of that flickering light?

On tiptoe now, Janey headed toward the living-room doorway, but she paused just short of it. She took a quick peek around the corner and into the room, then snapped back against the wall like a spy in a cartoon.

It was the TV. The TV had been left on.

But there was someone hunched over on the sofa.

Janey could not make sense of what she'd just seen, so she bit her lips tightly together—as if that might make her transparent—and peered around the corner once more.

It looked a little like Grandpa, only this was a Grandpa Janey had never seen before, or dreamed of seeing. It wasn't only that he was dressed in his paja-mas, although Janey had never seen him when he wasn't wearing regular clothes. And it wasn't simply that his hair was messed up, which it was.

But he was crying, almost silently. Sobs shook his body.

Crying.

Grandpa.

Back against the wall, Janey felt hot and cold at the same time. How totally embarrassing, she thought. What was she supposed to do? Should she run in and try to comfort him? Sneak into the bathroom, flush the toilet with the bathroom door open to warn him that someone was coming, and *then* go in and snuggle up with him, hoping that would make him feel better?

Or should she simply creep back to bed and pretend this whole thing had never happened?

Time seemed to slow down for Janey as she stood there with her back pressed against the wall. And then, it was as though she were watching a big ship turn around in the ocean: Slowly, slowly, her point of view shifted, and she saw the situation in a brand-new way.

The fact that she'd seen Grandpa crying was not something terrible that was happening to *her*, Janey realized. Or rather, that wasn't the important thing about it. What was worse was how Grandpa felt.

Was he crying because he knew now that he was going to have to keep on working forever, or at least until he could no longer hobble in to his shop?

Was he crying because his nice quiet house—well, as quiet as a house could be with Aunt Baby in it—

was now filled to the brim with YoYo and Janey? Or because he no longer had his study to retreat to when things got a little hairy with Aunt Baby?

No, Janey realized. He was crying because Poppy was dead.

Poppy. Peter. Petey, Grandpa's only child.

His little boy.

Janey knew for certain now that that was why Grandpa said things stunk.

She thought of her grandfather's back, so quickly glimpsed through the doorway. He had looked smaller than usual, wearing his light blue pajamas, and his hunched back looked distressingly bony and frail. Usually, when she hugged him it was like hugging a tree. She had never even thought of him as old, not really, in spite of what Aunt Baby said.

This Grandpa, though, looked more like a bunch of sticks someone had tied together and left standing too long in the wind.

Janey's hands formed fists that were closed so tightly, her fingernails cut into her palms.

Poor Grandpa, she thought, feeling as if something further had broken inside her.

She did not go to him, though, because—what was there to say?

CHAPTER SEVENTEEN

The Battle for YoYo

YoYo spent the entire next day doing things with Aunt Baby, no matter how hard Janey tried to get her to play. YoYo and Aunt Baby watched TV together, folded laundry, made tuna sandwiches for lunch that they cut out to look like stars, took a nap, and deadheaded flowers in the backyard garden. Janey watched them from afar, pretending to read.

Grandpa was at work, of course. But Janey understood better now why he fled there first thing each morning, before anyone else was awake.

She wanted to call Stacy, but she was afraid of running up a big long-distance bill and making things even worse for her grandfather. Besides, what if Mrs. Lindholm answered the phone and started grilling her about *feelings*?

When it was time to shop for dinner, Janey told

Aunt Baby that she'd prefer to stay home, but her great-aunt insisted that she accompany her to the store. YoYo was already waiting in the car, she said.

Janey sulked in the backseat of the car as Aunt Baby backed slowly out of the driveway and turned down Eucalyptus Terrace. "I don't see why I couldn't have just stayed home," she said. *Home.* Why had she said home? Janey felt like kicking herself.

Leroux Street was home. Eucalyptus Terrace *wasn't*.

"I stick out like a sore thumb, with all these bandages. And anyway, Mommy used to let me stay in my room and read whenever she went shopping," Janey added, hoping that might erase her use of the word.

"I doubt that very much," Aunt Baby said, not taking her eyes off the road.

Which was exactly the same thing as calling her a liar, Janey fumed silently.

"It's true," YoYo piped up, unexpectedly loyal. "Mommy did let her stay home when we went to the store."

"Well, I'm not her mommy," Aunt Baby snapped, stunning both of her passengers for a moment. "Now quiet down for a minute, you two. I need to make a left turn, and I have to concentrate."

* * *

Glendale was just dumb, Janey thought, glaring out the window. If they were even *in* Glendale anymore. Back home—her real home, Janey emphasized to herself—a person was either in Flagstaff or out of it. And if you went too far out of it, heading north, anyway, you might fall into the Grand Canyon.

But in Southern California, Janey had noticed during the long drive west, all the cities sort of blended together. Were you in Claremont or Pomona? Monrovia, Pasadena, Eagle Rock, or Glendale? They looked exactly the same, at least when you were in a car on the freeway, and there was no telling where one city ended and the next began.

No open spaces, only cities.

"Is this near where Grandpa works?" YoYo asked, peering around excitedly.

"No. His place is over by the river," Aunt Baby said.

"There's a river?" Janey asked skeptically, as a Wendy's and an Arby's slid by, followed by a KFC.

Did people do nothing out here but eat fast food all day long?

Aunt Baby nodded once, and her straight gray hair jiggled emphatically. "Mmm-hmm," she said.

"The Los Angeles River. But it doesn't have any water in it—at least not most of the time. It's just sort of a big storm drain now."

"Huh," Janey said scornfully.

The Colorado. Now, *there* was a river.

YoYo was thinking. "I don't think it can even *be* a river if it doesn't have any water," she finally said. "I think it's just a hole."

"Yeah. The Los Angeles Hole," Janey said from the backseat.

YoYo cackled appreciatively, and Janey felt close to her again, at least for the moment.

Really, this was kind of like playing Ping-Pong, Janey thought. First Aunt Baby got control of the ball—YoYo—and then she, Janey, did.

But who was going to win the battle for YoYo?

"We're here," Aunt Baby said, pulling into a shady spot in the supermarket parking lot.

"Do they have a candy machine inside?" YoYo asked.

Candy? "You're not allowed to eat candy, YoYo," Janey reminded her sister. "Not between meals, anyway. Except for the day after Halloween."

"But Aunt Baby lets me!" YoYo said, eyes wide.

"Sometimes," Aunt Baby confirmed reluctantly.

Janey took a deep breath. "Mommy doesn't allow us to eat candy whenever we happen to feel like it," she said.

Aunt Baby gave an exasperated shrug. "Well, I didn't know that, did I? YoYo certainly didn't tell me that when we were in Phoenix. She ate candy there like it was going out of style."

"I forgotted," YoYo said softly, babyishly. Pop went her thumb into her mouth.

"Mommy *hates* candy," Janey said, exaggerating a bit.

It was hot out, and beads of perspiration sparkled on her face, and Aunt Baby had had just about enough. "Well, Mommy doesn't have a vote anymore, does she?" she said, slamming the car door harder than was necessary. "Everything's all up to me!" Her face was pink as she grabbed a startled YoYo by the hand.

Mommy doesn't have a vote anymore.

Janey could not believe what she had just heard.

"Ouch?" YoYo said, making it a question as she tried to tug her arm away from Aunt Baby's grip.

Her little sister wasn't really hurt, though—Janey could tell. When YoYo was hurt, Mommy and Poppy always said, the whole world knew about it.

But who cared what Mommy and Poppy had always said?

Certainly not Aunt Baby, Janey thought bitterly, watching the sturdy figure march a still-complaining YoYo across a shimmering expanse of striped asphalt.

CHAPTER EIGHTEEN

Last Straw

They arrived home hot and still embarrassed by their fight to find piles of brand-new plastic-wrapped furniture on the front lawn, waiting to be assembled. Grandpa was supervising two men while they moved his old swivel rocker out the front door. A half-loaded pickup truck with BISHOP PLUMBING SUPPLY painted on the side sat waiting at the curb.

"Howard, *now*?" Aunt Baby exclaimed, clambering out of the car. Clearly, she had not been expecting this. She sounded as though she were about to burst into tears.

This must be that last straw everyone always talked about, Janey thought grimly.

"We left the driveway clear for you," Grandpa said, waving his hand in the air. "Remember Luis and Martin, from the shop?" he asked his sister, seeming silently to beg her to be polite.

The men inclined their heads graciously as they carried the rocker to the truck, but Aunt Baby was temporarily speechless.

Janey and YoYo got out of the car. Janey stretched, stiff from the ride, and YoYo scampered over to inspect Grandpa's purchases.

"Oh, honestly, Howard," Aunt Baby finally said, nearly snorting with exasperation. "Where are you going to put all your old stuff?"

"In the garage," Grandpa said, getting a couple of sacks of groceries out of the trunk. "Don't poke any holes in the plastic, YoYo," he called over to his granddaughter. "We have to put all that together, don't forget. I don't want to lose any of the pieces."

"Well, don't expect *me* to be able to do it," Aunt Baby said, thrusting a bag toward Janey. "The instructions are probably all in Swedish."

"Don't worry. Martin and Luis have done it before, they tell me," Grandpa reassured her.

"Everything's pure white," YoYo reported excitedly from the middle of the lawn.

"You have to help us carry in the groceries, YoYo," Janey called out.

"Oh," Aunt Baby said softly, "let her have a little fun."

✷ ✷ ✷

"You never liked my mom, did you?" Janey asked Aunt Baby almost casually after dinner. She was loading the dishwasher while Aunt Baby rinsed the dishes. Grandpa and the men from the shop were finishing assembling the new furniture in the girls' bedroom. Their occasional cries of triumph echoed down the hall.

Janey could hear YoYo yodeling in the bathroom. Her little sister's baths could last at least an hour, and tonight YoYo wanted to get sparkling clean, she'd told everyone, including the much-amused Martin and Luis, because she would be sleeping in her brand-new pure white bed.

"Goodness, Janey," Aunt Baby said, pausing for a moment, "where did *that* question come from?" She blinked her surprise and let warm water from the faucet wash over her temporarily idle hands.

Janey shrugged as if her question had just been answered, but she didn't meet Aunt Baby's startled gaze. "I knew it," she mumbled.

Aunt Baby turned off the water and reached for a dish towel to dry her hands. "I don't know what you think you know, young lady, but whatever it is, I've no doubt but that you've got it all wrong."

"Well, tell me the truth, then," Janey challenged her.

Aunt Baby shook her head slowly, as if astounded by Janey's nerve.

Janey was even more surprised. She could feel her heart pound.

But this was what had to be behind all that—that *spoiling* stuff Aunt Baby was doing with YoYo, Janey figured. Aunt Baby was just getting even with her mom in some sick way, or having the last word—or something. So why not call her on it?

Aunt Baby should at least admit it, if it was true. "You never liked her," Janey said again.

Aunt Baby reached blindly for a kitchen chair and lowered herself into it without looking. "We didn't ever fight," she said, not quite answering Janey's question.

"But you—"

"Let me finish," Aunt Baby said, holding up her hand. "We never really fought, but no, we did not get along particularly well."

Aha! "You didn't like her."

"Well, she didn't like me either, did you ever think about that?" Aunt Baby said, old hurt still showing in her eyes. "I tried to be friends with her, Janey. But oh no, she wanted you girls and your daddy all to herself. Which is how you all ended up in Flagstaff, of course. It just about broke your Grandpa's poor heart, too."

"La, la, la-a-a-a!" YoYo's voice—made hollow from the bathroom tile—floated down the carpeted hall and into the kitchen.

"I didn't know that," Janey said. "I don't think it's even true. You're lying."

Aunt Baby sighed. She looked tired—and old, Janey realized with a start. She looked every minute of her sixty-two years, and then some. She no longer looked like a person other people would ever dream of calling "Baby."

"It's not true," Janey repeated, although now she thought it might be.

"Do you remember that time a couple of years ago when Grandpa told your folks that he and I might just pack up and move to Flagstaff? Sell the business and the house and everything?"

Janey sat down, too. "Kind of," she admitted. "But nothing ever came of it."

"That's because your parents asked us not to come," Aunt Baby said softly. "I'm pretty sure that was mostly your mother's idea, though. I was just as glad, what with my altitude-sickness problem and everything."

Aunt Baby's story about almost moving didn't sound right to Janey. "Why would Mommy have cared if you moved to Flagstaff or not? You weren't going to live in our house with us or anything, were you?"

"No," Aunt Baby said. "Howard had his eye on a beautiful place out near the golf course."

"Then—"

"Norrie didn't have any other family, did she?" Aunt Baby interrupted. "Her folks were gone, and there were no brothers or sisters."

"That's right," Janey admitted.

"I think maybe she just didn't know how to share you with us," Aunt Baby said thoughtfully. "Oh, she didn't mind visits once or twice a year, but I'll bet she didn't really look forward to them."

Clear as water, Janey had a sudden memory of her mother sorting through clothes for the July trip west. "Maybe I'll give this to Aunt *Bay-bee*," she'd said, laughing, as she held up an oversized T-shirt against her own slim figure. She had made a comic face.

That hadn't been very nice, Janey thought reluctantly.

"I don't suppose I looked forward to those visits

much, either," Aunt Baby confessed. "I always loved seeing Peter again, though. And you and YoYo, of course."

"Yeah. But that's not the same thing as raising us, is it?"

Aunt Baby held very still. "No, it's not," she said.

The words that Aunt Baby had said to Ms. Ramiro in the Phoenix hospital room seemed still to ring in Janey's ears. "If you'd wanted kids, you would have had them, wouldn't you?" she asked Aunt Baby, repeating those very words.

Aunt Baby stood up so fast that her chair tipped over. "How—how dare you!" she barely managed to say.

Janey jumped to her feet, too. "How dare *you*?" she said, her voice shaking. "How dare you say bad stuff about Mommy and Poppy when they aren't even here to defend themselves? And how dare you try to spoil my little sister so much that they wouldn't even recognize her?"

YoYo appeared suddenly at the kitchen door, dripping wet and eyes wide. "I'm not spoiled!" she objected.

"Well, you're getting there, YoYo," Janey said, "with your candy, and your nasty white bread that Mommy hates, and—and stop *twirling your hair like that!*"

she scolded her sister, who promptly burst into tears.

"Stop it, stop it, stop it," YoYo screamed. "I want to go *home*!"

"Now look what you've done," Janey and Aunt Baby shouted at each other over YoYo's wails.

CHAPTER NINETEEN

Inside Out

All she had to do was to pick up the phone and call Dr. Vilner's pager number, Janey remembered much later that night, seated at her brand-new desk. Dr. Vilner was probably the only person in the world who could talk some sense into Aunt Baby.

And it was only eleven P.M., Janey told herself unconvincingly. Dr. Vilner looked as if she were a person who enjoyed staying up late. She was probably reading some interesting medical book right this very minute.

The only trouble was, what would happen after Janey paged her? Dr. Vilner would return the page, calling right back as promised, but that meant the phone would ring. And Aunt Baby would hear it. Maybe she'd even pick up the receiver.

Janey looked over at the gleaming top bunk where her sleeping sister lay sprawled in bed, looking as if she'd dropped there from the ceiling. Her little hand poked through the guardrail. YoYo's curls were still damp from her bath.

Aunt Baby had actually calmed YoYo down after the big blowup, Janey admitted to herself, even though Janey thought she, Janey, could have done the same thing. Faster, probably.

She knew YoYo best.

I'll take care of you, YoYo.

Janey reached for the phone. She *had* to call. She would pick up the phone the very second Dr. Vilner called back, she told herself. She lifted the receiver.

Someone was talking.

"Look, Reeny, she doesn't hate you," the voice was saying.

It—it sounded like Dr. Vilner! And "Reeny" was obviously Irene. Aunt Baby.

"You don't know," Aunt Baby said. "You've never heard the way she talks to me. Why can't she be more like YoYo? We get along so well!"

They were talking about *her*, Janey realized. Her stomach gave a little flip.

She knew she should hang up, but she couldn't. She tried to hold her breath.

"YoYo's not exactly in such great shape either," Dr. Vilner pointed out.

"But at least she likes me. At least I have a relationship with her," Aunt Baby said, sniffling a little.

"Of course you do," Dr. Vilner said. "She's only five, and you took care of her the whole time you were in Phoenix, didn't you?"

"You know I did."

"So naturally there's more of a bond."

"Which Janey is trying her darnedest to break," Aunt Baby said heatedly. "And it's YoYo who is paying the price."

"How do you mean?"

Aunt Baby sighed. "Well, you should just see the look on her face when Janey and I start squabbling over her," she said. "She's trying so hard to please us both that she's about to turn inside out, poor little thing."

Janey hoped that the beating of her heart was not as loud as it sounded in her ears. She had never thought of YoYo as being so—so *complicated*. Could Aunt Baby possibly be right about this?

She looked up at her sister, who twitched a little in her sleep.

"And what about Janey?" Dr. Vilner asked.

"What about her?" Aunt Baby asked, sounding bitter.

"You keep saying that she hates you, but I don't buy that. I think she's hurting just as much as YoYo is, only she doesn't know how to show it."

Hurting. Just as much as YoYo was.

"Janey doesn't understand how hard I'm trying!" Aunt Baby wailed.

"Now don't go feeling sorry for yourself, Irene," Dr. Vilner said, her voice firm.

"Well, why shouldn't I? *Your* world didn't turn upside down, did it? It was ours that did, mine and Howard's—and admit it, most of the work is falling to me. Howard's just barely holding it together."

"And you know you're going to buckle down and continue to do that work," Dr. Vilner told her briskly. "That's just the sort of person you are. Get some help in the house, if you need it."

"But help costs money, and we—"

"Oh, we're not talking about the money, and you know it," Dr. Vilner interrupted. "Howard has some money put aside, I'll bet—enough to tide you over until a judgment is reached. The lawsuit will be resolved one way or another, Reeny, but you're still going to be fighting with Janey however it turns out, if I know you. You just want somebody to blame for this whole sorry mess, someone to take things out on. And so does Janey, by the way! But she has an excuse—she's only twelve. Don't you think it's easier for her to battle with you than it is for her to miss her mom and dad? It's YoYo who's suffering most when you two fight, though, isn't it?"

"I suppose," Aunt Baby said reluctantly.

"Do you hate Janey, Irene?" Dr. Vilner asked after a moment.

"Of course not!"

"Now wait," Dr. Vilner said. "Don't answer so quickly. Think about it for a minute. Do you hate her?"

Janey bit her lip and tried again not to breathe.

"I don't have to think about it," Aunt Baby said. "I love that girl—and I always have, even though Norrie never gave us much of a chance to get close. Janey won't give me a break, though."

"Well, give *yourself* a break and go to bed," Dr. Vilner advised, laughing a little. "We'll talk later. You've got a long day ahead of you, most likely."

"You're right about that," Aunt Baby said, sounding worn out in advance. "Good night, Nancy. And thanks."

"'Night, Reeny."

Janey heard a click, breathed a relieved sigh, and started to hang up the phone.

"And good night to you, Janey," Dr. Vilner said.

Janey hesitated, then held the receiver to her hot ear once more. "How did you know?" she whispered.

"Heard you pick up," Dr. Vilner said, chuckling. "Don't worry, though. In her condition, your Aunt Baby didn't notice a thing."

"That's good," Janey said softly. "I—I'm sorry. I don't usually listen in."

"That's okay. It'll be our secret," Dr. Vilner said. "Good night, Janey," she repeated.

"Good night."

What if Aunt Baby *had* said she hated her when Dr. Vilner asked? Dr. Vilner was taking kind of a big chance, asking her great-aunt a question like that when she knew that she, Janey, was listening in, Janey thought a little indignantly as she shivered and gazed around the darkened room.

Dr. Vilner must have known what Aunt Baby's answer would be, Janey realized, much relieved.

But how did she, Janey, feel about Aunt Baby?

And what am I going to do about YoYo? Janey asked herself.

CHAPTER TWENTY

Reeny and Grandpoppy

Janey slept poorly that night; she didn't really fall asleep until after three A.M., and so she didn't hear YoYo get up the next morning. It was almost nine when she finally opened her eyes.

Ever since the accident, Janey had taken a silent roll call first thing each morning as a means of reminding herself of the way things were now:

Janey: *Present—sort of.*
YoYo: *Present, thank goodness.*
Grandpa and Aunt Baby: *Present.*
Mommy and Poppy: *Still absent.*

This morning, Janey ran through these familiar names in her head as she gazed up at the empty bed above her. She didn't mind sleeping in the bottom bunk, she decided. It was a little like being tucked away inside a cave.

Not that she'd had much choice.

Janey got up, dressed quickly, choosing her shorts and T-shirt from a stack of clean folded clothes Aunt Baby had left piled on a chair, and slipped silently out the door and into the hall. She heard the soft muffled sound of easy laughter; everyone seemed to be in the kitchen, in a good mood and lingering over their breakfast. She could smell toast.

"I'm the baby," she heard YoYo say as she neared the kitchen.

YoYo *was* the baby, Janey reminded herself. She was only five, after all. And—and perhaps she needed someone like Aunt Baby, who could pretend to be a mom, more than she needed a sister.

For now, anyway.

Even a not-so-great mom was better than no mom at all.

Maybe giving YoYo up was the best way she, Janey, could take care of her.

You win, Aunt Baby, Janey thought, and she could feel Mommy and Poppy slip away from her a little bit more even as her mind formed the words.

"And you be the mom, Aunt Baby," YoYo was saying

playfully, as if she had read Janey's thoughts.

Janey heard Aunt Baby laugh. It was a pretty, unfamiliar sound. "But *I've* always been the baby," she teased.

"No, you be the mom," YoYo said, more insistently this time. "We already have a baby in this family, and it's me. Remember?"

Unseen, Janey paused in the hallway, holding her breath.

She heard Grandpa rustle his newspaper. "Be the mom, Irene. Get it over with."

"O-o-okay," Aunt Baby said slowly. "But I want you to call me something else, YoYo. Because you already have a mom, don't forget. *Norrie,*" she added, as if reminding herself.

"I know, but she's not here right now," YoYo pointed out.

Janey sneaked a peek around the corner. YoYo was snuggled in Aunt Baby's lap at the kitchen table, melting into the woman's curves like a kitten. Aunt Baby looked softer, somehow; the usual ruler-straight line of her bangs was ruffled and uneven, her round face was free of makeup, and she was wearing navy-blue sweatpants and a faded red T-shirt rather than one of the fussy, too-tight outfits she usually favored.

She looked happy. Tired, but happy.

More important, so did YoYo.

Grandpa seemed happy, too, or at least not as sad as Janey had seen him be during the past month. The three of them looked almost like a real family.

She, Janey, was the only one goofing things up around here, Janey thought sadly. There was a hollow feeling inside her chest.

"I'll call you Irene, like Grandpa does," YoYo was saying.

"You'll do no such thing, young lady," Aunt Baby told her, drawing back in mock horror. "'Irene' is for when people are mad at me. You're not mad at me, are you?"

"No, I love you!"

"Call her Reeny," Grandpa suggested over the top of his newspaper. "She doesn't mind that."

"I'll be the baby, and you be the Reeny," YoYo said, delighted.

"I'll be the Reeny," Aunt Baby agreed. "Now finish your cereal, baby."

"Okay, Reeny."

Janey walked into the kitchen as if making an entrance onto a stage and kissed Grandpa's cheek.

"Darlin'," he said absentmindedly, giving her a crinkle-eyed smile over the top of his reading glasses.

YoYo and Aunt Baby looked startled, then a little guilty. "Good morning, Janey—let me fix you some breakfast," Aunt Baby said, jumping up and then plopping YoYo back onto the kitchen chair.

"That's okay. I'm just having cereal. I can get it," Janey said, getting down a bowl.

"I'm calling Aunt Baby 'Reeny' now," YoYo announced, her voice a little too loud. She sounded brave and scared at the same time, as though she was thinking that maybe she should have first gotten Janey's permission to change Aunt Baby's name.

"That's good," Janey said, carefully pouring cereal into her bowl. She did not look at Aunt Baby, though.

Because wasn't it enough that her great-aunt had won the battle for YoYo?

Aunt Baby had won, and she, Janey, had lost.

She'd lost her parents.

She'd lost her two best friends.

She'd lost her hometown, and her house, and her pale violet bedroom.

She'd even lost her face, or at least the top layer of

it. There was almost no part of her original face left that her mother and father had kissed.

And now, Janey thought bleakly, she had given up her little sister. But at least she'd had a choice this time, and she had made that choice out of love.

"YoYo wants to be the baby for a while," Aunt Baby said, as if she felt she had to offer an explanation. She busied herself at the sink.

"Oh," Janey said politely. "Please pass the sugar." She glanced at her little sister. Did being the baby mean that YoYo was going to be sucking her thumb and twirling her hair all the time now?

But no. There was no sucking or twirling going on. YoYo simply watched her, a questioning look in her eyes.

"What?" Janey said, irritated.

"Will you call her Reeny, too?" YoYo asked.

"She doesn't have to," Aunt Baby said quickly from the sink.

"So, YoYo, what are you going to call me now?" Grandpa asked, probably to change the subject.

"Grandpoppy," YoYo said promptly, and Janey's heart seemed to twist a little more.

But why shouldn't that be her grandfather's new name, if he had to have one? she asked herself. Grandpa was Poppy's father. The name *Grandpoppy* made sense.

"What do you think about that, Janey?" Grandpa asked, giving his oldest granddaughter his full attention.

"I like it," Janey said, trying to sound enthusiastic.

"Reeny and Grandpoppy, Grandpoppy and Reeny," YoYo chanted, satisfied. "But we *all* have to call them that," she added, suddenly strict.

Janey longed to give a sarcastic shrug, at the very least, to demonstrate exactly how far removed she felt from what was going on. But instead, she nodded. "Okay," she said. She started to eat her cereal.

And then the phone rang.

CHAPTER TWENTY-ONE

But Where Are They?

"It's Arnold Chesterton," Grandpa—Grandpoppy—mouthed, his hand over the receiver mouthpiece.

Mr. Chesterton. Their Phoenix attorney.

Janey carefully placed her spoon in the bowl of mostly uneaten cereal.

"Take the call in your study," Aunt Baby said. Reeny now.

But Grandpoppy didn't have a study anymore.

"Hold on a minute, I'm going upstairs," Grandpoppy told Mr. Chesterton. He handed Reeny the receiver. "Hang up for me, would you?" he said.

Reeny held the telephone receiver as if it were an unfamiliar but valuable object, containing Mr. Chesterton on the other end as it did, and Janey watched her.

The lawsuit. Reporters. The hospital.

The cold hot Arizona desert.

Was Reeny going to start acting like Aunt Baby again? Excited and angry, wearing too much makeup and issuing statements to the press?

YoYo was watching Aunt Baby, too. She isolated a strand of hair above her left ear and began to fiddle with it.

The faucet dripped, the kitchen clock ticked, and Reeny—hearing Grandpoppy start to talk upstairs— hung up the phone. "Well then," she said uncertainly, looking around the kitchen, "where were we? YoYo, baby, don't do that."

"Family meeting in the living room in five min- utes," Grandpoppy announced about an hour later, sticking his head into the room Janey shared now with YoYo.

Family meeting. Poppy used to say that. He'd probably gotten it from his father, Janey realized.

YoYo was out back helping Reeny in the garden. The little girl had asked Janey if she wanted to play Barbies with her, but Janey said she wanted to read.

Reeny had looked both startled and relieved, hearing this.

"I'll go tell the others," Grandpoppy said to Janey, and he disappeared.

Janey put down the book she'd been pretending to read and stood up. It was as though her legs were weighted with sand, however.

Sand. How weird, she thought dully.

She forced those legs to move her down the hall and into the living room. Grandpoppy was already there. She could hear YoYo and Reeny washing their hands in the kitchen. "Where do you want me to sit?" she asked Grandpoppy, feeling shy.

Grandpoppy glanced up from the notes he'd taken while on the phone with Mr. Chesterton. "Oh, anywhere," he said, surprised. "How about that chair over there?"

Relieved to have the decision made for her, Janey lowered herself onto what was really an extra dining-room chair. She felt as though she were watching herself from across the room.

"We're here!" YoYo said, bursting into the room and flinging herself onto the sofa. Reeny sat down next to her and smiled tentatively at Janey.

Grandpoppy cleared his throat as though about to address a large crowd of people. Poppy had always done the same thing, Janey remembered.

"That was Mr. Chesterton on the phone," Grandpoppy began—unnecessarily, in Janey's opinion, since they already knew that.

"And?" Reeny said, eager.

"And the criminal proceedings against Mrs. Sandor are almost done, except for the sentencing."

"Who's Mrs. Sandor?" YoYo asked, confused.

Reeny hugged her tight. "She's the woman who—who—"

"She's the drunk driver who killed Mommy and Poppy," Janey said coolly, remembering the woman's name from the taped interview in her hospital room.

"That's right," Grandpoppy said, and he cleared his throat. "The investigators who testified at the criminal trial said there was nothing wrong with either the road or her car, and she failed the Breathalyzer test, and there were witnesses. So it was determined that the accident was entirely her fault."

"Accident," Reeny snorted, still holding YoYo in a bear hug. "I'm surprised she even let them give her that test. Didn't she scream for a fancy lawyer to come rescue her?"

"You don't have much choice about taking the test, not in Arizona," Grandpoppy said. "They don't mess around, no matter how much money you have or who your husband is. They automatically take away your driver's license for a year if you refuse to take the test. Her alcohol concentration was 0.21," he added, disgusted. "And in Arizona, anything 0.18 or more qualifies as the highest level of intoxication."

"What's going to happen to her?" Janey asked.

"It looks like she's going to be spending some time behind bars, I'm happy to say," Grandpa replied. "The judge hasn't made his final ruling yet, Mr. Chesterton says, but she's facing more than thirty-nine years in prison," he added, consulting his notes. "Two manslaughter convictions at twelve and a half years each, one aggravated assault conviction of twelve and a half years for hurting Janey, and one endangerment conviction of one and a half years for almost hurting YoYo. And then there's that man who got injured trying to help."

"It serves her right," YoYo said, glowering.

"And she'll probably be fined, too," Grandpoppy said, "but I think one hundred thousand dollars is the Arizona limit in the criminal trial."

One hundred thousand dollars sounded like a lot of money to Janey.

"Chicken feed," Reeny murmured, hugging YoYo once more.

"Chicken feed," YoYo echoed, liking the words.

"We'll be filing our civil suit against her in a few weeks," Grandpoppy concluded.

The room was silent for a moment, and then Reeny spoke. "The real question is, how much is Mr. Chesterton going to sue that woman *for* in the civil trial?"

"Well, he's still figuring that out," Grandpoppy told her. "But it will be a substantial amount."

"Substantial" meant "a lot." Janey knew that much.

"How much?" Reeny asked again.

Grandpoppy sighed. "He has to take a lot of things into account to come up with an amount of money he can defend in court. You don't just make up any old number."

"But what if Mrs. Sandor doesn't have very much money left, after paying that other fine?" Janey asked.

"Now, don't you go feeling sorry for her," Reeny scolded, squeezing YoYo tight.

"Well, Janey doesn't have to feel sorry for Mrs. Sandor," Grandpoppy said, "because it's not very likely that much of the civil-suit judgment money will come out of her pocket—or her husband's. Their insurance company will have to pay if we win. And pay big-time. The Sandors will have to pay what their insurance doesn't cover, though."

So, this *was* about the money, Janey thought. But so what? Why shouldn't it be? People—kids, especially— needed money to live.

And money was the easiest thing to measure. How much would her parents have made during their life-times? How expensive had Janey's medical care been? How much was college for Janey and YoYo going to cost?

You could add it all up.

"That's not fair," YoYo said, giving the sofa a kick. "They should take all the money out of her allowance!"

Janey nearly laughed out loud—but she agreed with YoYo, in a way. Because if it wasn't going to real-ly, really hurt Mrs. Sandor to pay, why bother suing her?

Why bother, except to make things easier for Grandpoppy—and for Reeny, too, with a bigger house, maybe, and some help in running it? And then there would be the possibility of retirement for Grandpoppy after all, and so on.

And money might make life easier for YoYo.

But she, Janey, didn't want a penny of Mrs. Sandor's nasty money. She just wanted Mommy and Poppy back.

"That would be some swell allowance," Reeny said.

"Mr. Chesterton says that her insurance company is going to want to settle with us," Grandpoppy informed them, flipping to the end of his notes.

"What does that mean?" Janey asked.

"It means they're scared to death that a jury will hear the case," Reeny said, shooting Grandpoppy a triumphant look.

"Scared to death," YoYo whispered, and Reeny looked abashed.

"In this case, 'settling' means that we would accept the money that the insurance company offered to keep the case from going to trial," Grandpa explained.

"And are we going to do that?" Janey asked.

"Probably not. We'll talk about it first, of course. But we'll listen to whatever Mr. Chesterton has to say, because that's why we hired him. Of course, he'll get part of any money we're awarded. Roughly one-third, in fact."

"How come?" YoYo asked indignantly. "It wasn't *his* mommy and daddy who got hurt, was it?"

Grandpoppy's smile was almost a grimace. "No, it wasn't," he said. "But we needed someone good to fight for you two kids, someone who'd be right there on the spot in Phoenix."

"On top of things," Reeny added.

"Mr. Chesterton came highly recommended," Grandpoppy assured Janey.

"Oh," Janey said. Like she cared.

YoYo thought for a moment, chewing her lower lip. "Does this mean we can go back home and see Mommy and Poppy now?" she finally asked.

Janey listened to her heart beat: One, two, three.

YoYo was five years old. Didn't she know what *dead* meant?

But why should she? Janey asked herself suddenly. Because of Poppy's allergies, their family had never had a pet, and so YoYo had never buried a hamster, even. And certainly no one they'd ever known in Flagstaff had died.

"Your Mommy and Poppy are dead, honey. You know that," Reeny said softly.

YoYo scowled. "Yeah, but I want to go see them."

"They're *dead*," Grandpoppy said, as if hearing the words from another voice might better convince the child.

"But where are they?" YoYo asked, sounding younger by the minute.

"YoYo doesn't know what *dead* means," Janey announced formally, thinking that her voice seemed as though it were traveling across a great distance. "See," she explained, "we never had anyone die before. And she didn't go to the funeral. How *could* she know?"

"I do too know what *dead* means," YoYo objected hotly, jumping off the sofa. "It's like at Halloween, with ghosts and stuff."

"It's *not* like at Halloween," Janey told her. "It's nothing like Halloween."

"Then where are they?"

"They're buried in the ground, YoYo—at the cemetery in Flagstaff," Grandpoppy said, scooping the little girl into his arms. "I went there myself, right after the funeral service at the church."

"I want to go see them," YoYo repeated, burrowing her head against his shoulder. "I want my Mommy! I want my Poppy!"

CHAPTER TWENTY-TWO

No Extra Charge

It was August twentieth, and this time the Bishops flew to Phoenix. Janey had never ridden in a plane before, so she couldn't help but be excited.

YoYo couldn't believe she was actually on an airplane. She got the window seat, naturally. Janey sat next to her, while Reeny and Grandpoppy sat across the aisle.

YoYo was not wearing her miracle clothes, thank goodness, although Reeny had looked tempted when YoYo raised the subject. "There won't be any reporters this trip, Irene," Grandpoppy said firmly. "They've moved on to the next tragedy."

Janey was glad to hear it. Apart from not wanting YoYo to act like a brat again, she didn't like the idea of her family's misery being some stranger's morning entertainment, the sad story read aloud while the listener munched his cornflakes.

YoYo was disappointed about the clothes, but she got over it.

After buckling her seat belt, Janey took a deep shaky breath and kicked her backpack under the seat in front of her as if she'd done it a hundred times. She touched the three gauze bandages that covered the worst of her remaining wounds—the rest of her face simply looked either badly sunburned or acne-ridden—and was thankful that no one at the Hollywood-Burbank Airport had seemed to find anything too unusual in her appearance. So maybe no one in Flagstaff would, either.

She settled back to enjoy every moment of the flight. "I don't really want to go," she remembered telling Dr. Vilner, "but I guess it will be good for YoYo."

"I think it'll be good for all four of you," Dr. Vilner had said.

Boris had been the one who'd objected to the trip. "You won't come back, I just know it," he'd said, flopping onto the grass in his backyard.

"Why do you say that?" Janey asked, her heart seeming to give a little jump. Had Boris heard someone say that they might be moving back to Flagstaff?

Grandpoppy, Reeny, YoYo, and her, Janey?

But how would she feel about such a move?

Not good, Janey had answered silently, surprising herself. Because while Glendale did not yet feel like home, Flagstaff wasn't home anymore, either. Not without Mommy and Poppy there.

Lying on the grass, Boris shook his head. "No reason," he said gloomily. "It would be just my luck to have my only friend on the street move away, that's all. And right before school starts, too."

Janey felt like giving her lonely neighbor's sneakered foot a reassuring squeeze, but she restrained herself. There was no point in grossing him out by getting all mushy. "We're not even going to be in the same grade at school," she reminded him instead.

"I know that," Boris said. "But it would have been cool to have someone to hang out with *after* school. We could have played my new video game instead of doing our homework."

"Well, I'm coming back," Janey said. "Do you actually think I'd move away before you had a chance to show me the shortcuts on those tracks you're going to teach me?" she asked, referring to the game's most advanced levels.

Boris sat up, his face brightening. "Do you mean it?" he asked.

"Yeah," Janey had told him. "We'll just be gone for a few days. I promise."

The plane lifted off, circled over some mountains, and then headed east. Janey and YoYo held hands during the takeoff. "There goes Glendale," YoYo said, trying to look down past the wing.

"Yeah," Janey whispered. "There goes Glendale."

It was hard to believe. Grandpoppy had arranged to rent a car in Phoenix, and they were going to drive up to Flagstaff. They'd be arriving that very evening. Grandpoppy, Reeny, and YoYo were going to stay at a bed-and-breakfast. Janey was going to stay with the Lindholms.

She was nervous about seeing Stacy again, but relieved that she wouldn't have to be crammed into yet another strange bedroom with YoYo.

Stacy. "Don't invite everybody over, okay?" Janey had asked her friend when they finally talked on the phone. *Everybody*, meaning Ramona. "There's a lot of stuff my family has to do, remember."

Janey felt disloyal to Mommy and Poppy when she called Grandpoppy and Reeny "my family." But what else could she call them?

The Flagstaff plan was simple: The Bishops would

bring flowers to the cemetery first thing the next morning, take a few pictures of the marker, read YoYo the words on it, and try to get her to realize that Mommy and Poppy were gone forever. Then they would attempt to enjoy the rest of their brief visit, drive back down to Phoenix, and fly back to Burbank.

Janey wondered if Stacy was really glad that she was coming. She hoped so. It had been weird, just disappearing from each other's life the way they had.

Moving away from friends—especially suddenly—had to be one of the worst things about being a kid.

"Janey, do you know what's down there?" YoYo whispered urgently, pointing toward the window as she clasped Birdy to her chest with her other hand.

Janey craned her neck and tried to look out, but YoYo had steamed the window up with her breath. "No, what?" she asked.

"The world," YoYo said, thrilled, and Janey's heart seemed to melt as she squeezed her little sister's hand.

There was some trouble at the car rental desk; the only vehicle left was a white Mustang convertible. "That's not the car I ordered," Grandpoppy complained, frowning.

"I'm giving it to you at no extra charge," the rental

car woman said, her floppy bow tie almost quivering with indignation.

"But it's over one hundred degrees outside," Reeny said, fanning herself with a brochure. "We'll get sunstroke!"

"The top's up," the woman said. "And there's air-conditioning."

"We should just take it," Janey whispered to Grandpoppy. "Let's get out of here." They had a three-hour drive ahead of them.

Grandpoppy nodded, giving Janey the final word on the matter, and soon they were on Highway I-17, heading north to Flagstaff. He drove, and Reeny napped, exhausted, as though she'd been directly responsible for keeping their plane in the air. YoYo sucked her thumb as she gazed out the backseat window, but Janey didn't say anything about it for once.

She thought about Flagstaff, about their old house. Would Grandpoppy make her go see it? Walk through its empty rooms, even? She hoped not.

The house was still officially on the market, as the realtor put it, but an offer had been made. Pretty soon, some other family would be calling it home. They might even have a kid who would find the names Janey and her friends had printed on the underside of the lowest built-in shelf in her closet during one especially wild sleepover.

Jeremy, Nathan, Tyler.

Old secrets.

Visiting their empty house would almost be creepier than going to the cemetery, in Janey's opinion—even though she understood why they had to do *that*.

The visit to the cemetery was for YoYo.

Janey's thoughts turned to her parents. She tried to think of the *bad* things about them—because they hadn't been perfect, she kept reminding herself. Mommy could be impatient, short-tempered at times. She slammed doors when she got mad, and when she did, the whole family cringed.

She could be a little selfish, too. Look at how mean she'd always acted about Reeny. And Reeny was okay, really—not great, but okay. She was trying, at least.

And Poppy? He often put off doing stuff he didn't feel like doing, such as returning library books on time or going to the cleaners. Janey hated it when he was the one who was supposed to pick her up after a club meeting; it was almost a sure bet that he'd be late.

Losing them would be so much easier if she could hate them. They were *bad, bad*! she thought, trying out the idea.

No they weren't, she answered herself silently. They were just regular people, that's all. She loved them.

And every leaf on every tree in Flagstaff would probably remind her of them.

As if objecting to her earlier negative thoughts, YoYo—who had fallen asleep, in spite of her excitement—gave a yelp as she woke up. "What's the matter?" Janey asked, keeping her voice low.

"I had a scary dream," YoYo mumbled, sagging into sleep once more.

Her sister had probably already forgotten all the bad stuff about Mommy and Poppy, Janey thought, feeling a little bit jealous. She would always remember their parents as being perfect.

Lucky YoYo.

A couple of hours later, the road had risen through national forest past the five thousand–foot mark, well on its way to Flagstaff's altitude of seventy-five hundred feet. Pine trees seemed to grow taller with each mile as the Mustang neared Janey's hometown.

They pulled into a Mobil station half an hour south of Flagstaff to use the rest room. The sun was low in the sky, shadows were long, and it had cooled down enough to lower the convertible roof. "We're going to enter Flagstaff in style," Grandpoppy told his passengers with a grin.

"I wish I'd thought to bring a scarf," Reeny fretted, smoothing down her hair in advance, but she couldn't hide her look of pure pleasure.

Wide-awake and refreshed from their brief stop, YoYo bounced up and down with excitement. "It'll be just like we're in a parade," she exclaimed.

Janey simply felt exposed—and a little grouchy, although she tried to hide her feelings. She was having trouble joining in the fun.

But were they *supposed* to be having fun? Just because you got to ride in an airplane and in a convertible on the same day didn't mean you were having the vacation of a lifetime.

They were here to visit her parents' graves, for crying out loud.

CHAPTER TWENTY-THREE

Full Moon

Janey saw the sober little sign just after they reached the southernmost outskirts of the city: CEMETERY, 1.5 MILES. "Turn here," she told Grandpoppy suddenly.

And he did turn, without saying a word.

"Wait a sec," Reeny said, looking up from the map she'd unfolded back at the Mobil station. "We're not on Milton anymore. This isn't the way to Leroux Street."

"I—I want to see the cemetery now," Janey heard herself say.

Reeny tried to turn around so she could look at Janey. "But Janey, honey, I thought we were going there tomorrow. We don't even have any flowers with us."

"That's okay," Grandpoppy told his sister. "We'll come back tomorrow with the flowers."

Reeny turned to look at him, a question in her eyes, then shrugged a little. "All right," she said, "but it's almost dark out. The cemetery might not even be open."

It was, though, and Grandpoppy knew exactly where to go after driving through the black iron gates. He turned right and headed slowly down a narrow lane as the sky turned a deep violet. A full moon seemed to pop up heavy and golden over the cluster of fir trees that encircled the closely mown lawns. The air smelled like sweet hay.

"This doesn't look like a graveyard to me," YoYo said, looking around. She sounded disapproving.

"Well, it is," Grandpoppy said flatly.

"He's been here before, YoYo," Janey told her sister.

"But where are all the round things that are supposed to stick up out of the ground?" YoYo asked.

Actually, Janey thought, she, too, had been expecting to see tombstones—like they showed in scary old movies and on Halloween cards.

"This is a modern cemetery," Grandpoppy told YoYo. "They try to make these places look more like parks, nowadays. Not that it fools anyone," he added, speaking to himself.

"Well, that's just dumb," YoYo said. "A park has to have swings and stuff, so this isn't a park. And besides, how can you tell who's who if there's nothing sticking up?"

"They make special plaques that lie flat on the ground," Grandpoppy said. "I got a nice one made for your mom and dad, honey. It should be installed by now."

Janey looked around. Set into the grass, a few plaques glinted and winked in what was left of the light. The only other grave decorations were bunches of flowers—both real and plastic—that seemed to be plugged into the ground, a scattering of little American flags, and a few teddy bears propped up here and there.

Janey didn't even want to think about *that*, but once she started to, she couldn't stop: There could so easily have been a sun-bleached teddy bear left lolling on YoYo's grave, if things had gone only a tiny bit differently.

Or one could be lying on her own grave.

Who did that drunk driver think she *was*?

Was she even sorry?

Oh, not sorry that she'd gotten caught, but really and truly sorry for what she had done to Janey's family?

Janey could barely catch her breath, so great was her rage.

YoYo was twirling her hair again. "I don't like this place," she announced.

"Here we are," Grandpoppy said, pulling the car to the side of the narrow road and parking it.

"Who lives in that little house over there?" YoYo asked suspiciously, eyeing a small nearby structure.

"There's a faucet and some trash bins inside," Grandpoppy said. "It's so folks can fix up the flowers they've brought."

"Huh," YoYo said. "I'm not going in there."

"You don't have to. Everybody out of the car," Grandpoppy said.

Even though this evening's crazy expedition had been her own idea, Janey now wished she were any- where else but here. What in the world had she been *thinking*?

"Here we go," Reeny said, holding out her hand.

Janey let herself be pulled from the Mustang; the backs of her legs stuck to the seat a little. It was still that warm out.

"Come on, YoYo," Grandpoppy was saying. "I want to show you where your mother and father are buried."

Reluctant, YoYo allowed herself to be led to a spot near a split-rail fence that glowed almost white under the moonlight.

No, no, no, Janey thought.

But she let Reeny tug her over to the fence.

"Here they are," Grandpoppy said, gesturing down at a patch of grass. "I'll read the plaque to you, YoYo.

"PETER WALLACE BISHOP—
BORN SEPTEMBER 30, 1965, DIED JULY 2, 2001.
NORRIS HAWORTH BISHOP—
BORN APRIL 2, 1966, DIED JULY 2, 2001.
DEATH SHALL NOT PART THEM."

Reeny dug into her pocket, searching for a Kleenex.

Mommy used to use a handkerchief, Janey thought, numb.

Don't leave me, Poppy. You said that you never would.

Hold out your arms, Mommy—let me hug you one more time.

Please?

She swayed on her feet.

"But I don't get it," YoYo was saying in the cranky

tone she used when a joke went way over her head. "Why does that piece of metal on the ground have Mommy and Poppy's names on it?"

"Because that's where they're buried," Grandpoppy said, his voice cracking.

"Oh, Howard, this must be breaking your heart," Reeny said, and she blew her nose with a loud honk.

"But I don't get it," YoYo said again. "You mean they're in the *ground*?" She sounded angry now, and confused. She kicked at the grass a little.

Suddenly, it was all too much for Janey. "They're in the ground, they're in the ground, they're in the ground!" she yelled.

"Janey, don't," Reeny said, sounding scared. She looked around as if hoping Dr. Vilner might suddenly materialize—with one of her calming-down pills, perhaps.

"Let her shout," Grandpoppy told Reeny. "Let her."

"*Really?*" YoYo asked, hearing only Janey. She looked down at the grass beneath her feet and stepped back. Eyes wide and round face as pale as the moon, she looked as though she was finally beginning to believe what everyone had been telling her.

Janey dropped to her knees on her parents' graves

and took her little sister's icy hands in her own. "We're never going to see them again, YoYo," she whispered. "Never."

"Maybe in heaven," Reeny said, clasping her hands together.

"But—but I need them *now*," YoYo wailed.

For Janey, it was as though her sister's piercing cry caused the purple sky to shatter into a hundred pieces and fall to the ground.

Mommy and Poppy were dead.
Mommy and Poppy were dead.
Mommy and Poppy were dead.

"I need them, too, YoYo," she said, and finally— finally!—Janey Bishop began to cry.

Chapter Twenty-Four

Fine

Stacy Lindholm stood silhouetted at her front door as the Bishops' rented Mustang drove up San Francisco Street and pulled over to the curb. "Janey," she shouted, running to the side of the car. "I was so worried. I thought—I thought maybe you guys got lost or something," she gabbled, practically hauling Janey out of the backseat in her relief.

"Don't worry, I'm fine," Janey whispered, hugging her.

Janey's eyes were red, and her face was swollen from her tears, but she *was* fine, she thought, surprised. Or at least she was getting there.

"I told you they were all right, Stace," Mrs. Lindholm said, coming up behind the two girls. "Hello, darling," she murmured, giving Janey a warm squeeze. "You're looking so much better."

At least *Mrs. Lindholm* had stopped crying, Janey thought, relieved. She'd been kind of worried that Stacy's mother might greet her clutching that same soggy handkerchief she'd brought with her to the hospital that awful day.

"Thanks. And thank you for having me," Janey told Mrs. Lindholm—and Stacy.

"I want to go to our fancy hotel," YoYo called out, bouncing impatiently in the car. She seemed to have recovered—at least temporarily—from her trip to the cemetery, having finally decided that what Mommy and Poppy's graves really needed were some stuffed animals. It would make them look more *fun*, she declared. And she, YoYo, was going to select the perfect ones!

Maybe she'd get an extra toy for herself, she'd added quickly, just to get everyone used to the idea in advance.

"It's not a fancy hotel, YoYo. It's just a bed-and-breakfast place," Reeny tried to tell her as Grandpoppy shook hands with Mrs. Lindholm and then opened the trunk to get out Janey's duffel bag.

"Let's go, let's go, let's go," YoYo said, ignoring Reeny as she bounced.

"Bye, YoYo. See you after breakfast tomorrow,"

Janey called out as the Mustang pulled away.

But her little sister's reply, if there was one, was lost in the warm evening air.

Twelve, thirteen, fourteen. There *were* fourteen steps that led up to the Lindholms' third floor.

She'd been right.

Janey set her duffel bag on the bedroom floor and looked around as Stacy turned on a few lights. "Finally," Stacy said, turning around. She looked almost as shy as Janey felt.

"Finally," Janey agreed. "Thanks for writing me that letter," she added.

"Thank you for reading it," Stacy said, blushing a little.

This conversation was *not* making any sense, Janey thought, feeling excited, tired, and grouchy all at the same time. It was worse than talking to a stranger, and Stacy was no stranger. She was *Miney*, one of Janey's very best friends.

Or she had been, anyway.

Janey sat down on Stacy's guest bed and bounced up and down a little, the way YoYo had in the backseat of the car. "So, are you and Ramona still fighting?" she asked, staring with interest at a pale blue wall—as if something on its blank surface fascinated her.

"Not so much," Stacy said, shrugging. She folded her lanky frame onto the floor in a cross-legged sitting position.

Could Stacy have grown even taller? And her hair was longer, too, Janey noticed. It didn't look so strange anymore.

"We made up," Stacy said. "Nobody said they were sorry, though," she added.

"Huh."

"We couldn't," Stacy elaborated, as though Janey had asked for an explanation. "Because we couldn't even remember what the fight was about. I guess we were just kind of messed up for a while—about your parents, and you, and everything."

"Huh." Janey chewed on her lower lip for a moment. "So, doesn't she even want to see me?" she asked, finally looking at Stacy.

"Of *course* she does!" Stacy exclaimed. "I thought you told me you didn't want to see her! You said not to invite anybody over."

"I didn't mean Eeny," Janey said, not quite telling the truth.

She *hadn't* wanted to see Ramona, though, because—because, why try to recapture the past? And besides, she'd felt embarrassed by the way she looked.

But she felt different, now that she was actually back in Flagstaff.

Now that she had been to the cemetery.

She felt different, period.

Stacy was already halfway to the phone. "She's waiting for me to call her," she told Janey, laughing. "I was supposed to do it when you were taking a shower, or something."

"Is she still mad at me?" Janey asked. She felt nervous, because Ramona might be tiny, but she knew how to hold a grudge.

"Nuh-uh," Stacy told her, pressing one of her speed-dial buttons. "She wanted to write you, but she was too chicken. She was scared about seeing you, too."

I used to be on her speed dial, Janey thought, feeling a little bit sad.

But then, she also used to be a kid whose parents were alive.

She used to be a lot of things.

Hours later, all three girls were stretched out on the floor in sleeping bags in Stacy's darkened playroom. The room's paneled walls seemed cozy, even in the moonlight, and Janey let out a happy, nostalgic sigh.

She wondered, though, just for a moment, what good old Boris was doing.

Boris Morris. She was not going to try to explain *him* to Stacy and Ramona. Especially not Ramona, who would simply never understand why Janey might like hanging out with a ten-year-old video game addict who didn't seem to have any other friends and who had been born in Russia.

But Janey liked Boris. He was so far removed from any trace of her old life that she found it restful just being near him.

Besides, he did a really funny imitation of Aunt Baby. Of Reeny.

Maybe she could get Boris to consider changing his name—his school name, anyway—to Stevie, as his American parents had suggested.

Or Steve. That would be even better; he might make friends a little more easily with a more ordinary name.

Boris could still be his middle name, though. And she would always call him that.

But not talking to Stacy and Ramona about Boris was okay, Janey thought—because her two old friends probably had some new things in their lives that they weren't telling her. Or telling each other, for that matter.

That's just what happened sometimes.

"I'm so-o-o glad your face is going to be okay," Ramona said in her whispery voice.

"Me, too," Janey admitted.

"Are you scared about the operation?"

"A little."

"I guess you were lucky," Stacy said. "That's what my mom says, anyway."

A startled silence seemed to make the darkness quiver around the three girls.

Lucky?

"I guess," Janey agreed, not wanting to start an argument.

The playroom was silent for one or two long minutes. "Do you ever dream about them, Janey?" Ramona asked, her voice even softer than usual.

Janey sighed once more. "I don't know," she finally replied. "I think I do. I wake up happy, anyway, so I must have been dreaming about them."

"What was the last thing your mother and father said to you, do you remember?" Stacy asked, sounding almost as breathless as Ramona. "What were their final words?"

"Stacy!" Ramona chided her.

"No, that's okay," Janey told them both. "It's just

that I can't really *remember* their final words. The doctors said that's perfectly normal after such a bad accident, though."

Ms. Ramiro had told her that maybe she'd remember, someday.

"I'll bet they told you how much they loved you," Ramona said, hugging herself in the dark.

"Yeah," Stacy agreed in a husky voice.

"It was probably something like that," Janey said, just to make them feel better.

Now Ramona was the one to sigh. "That is so sad."

"No, it's not," Janey said. "I don't think that would be a sad thing at all for them to have said to me."

I just hope those were my last words to them, she added silently.

This time, a respectful silence filled the room.

"What was it like, Janey—out there in the desert that night?" Stacy asked.

"She told you," Ramona scolded. "She can't remember a thing."

"I do remember a few things," Janey said. "I remember the sand was cold. . . ."

Getting Ready to Leave

"Are those soda cans cold enough?" Norrie Bishop called into the garage. "Because there's no point bringing them with us in the car if the soda is going to taste like soup."

"Ginger ale soup," her husband Peter said to his daughter Janey as she handed him her sister YoYo's little pink suitcase. "Delicious!" He rolled his eyes, trying to make her laugh.

But Janey was having none of that. She was furious with her parents for making her go with them to California. Why couldn't she stay in Flagstaff, for once? Just because *they* felt obligated to make the trip to see Grandpa and Aunt Baby each year, that didn't mean Janey had to go, too, did it? Especially when it was almost the Fourth of July—and almost her birthday!

She'd be turning twelve on July sixth, and being twelve was the next best thing to being a teenager. Would they expect her to go everywhere with them when she was thirteen, too? And fourteen, and fifteen?

Really, her parents were just impossible.

She was almost twelve, and she was still calling them *Mommy* and *Poppy*. What was up with that? The familiar names were beginning to sound funny to Janey lately.

There were going to have to be some changes made around here, she vowed silently.

It was so unfair! Hadn't Stacy Lindholm's parents *said* they would take her, Janey, with them on their camping trip up Oak Creek Canyon? Now Stacy and Ramona would get to have all the fun, while she sat in the backseat of the Toyota with annoying YoYo for about a million years.

"Janey?" her father was asking.

"What?"

Poppy drew back in mock horror. "Gee, don't bite my head off," he told her. "I was just asking you to hand me your little sister's squashy pillow, that's all."

Janey blushed, feeling guilty. This mess wasn't Poppy's fault, after all. He would have gone along with whatever his wife said, usually leaving the nuts and bolts of parenting to her, as he did.

And Norrie Bishop said Janey was going with them to California. Period.

"YoYo's going to want that pillow with her in the car," Janey reminded her father, just as he was about to stuff it into a corner of the already-crowded trunk.

"Good point," he said, handing it to Janey to put in the backseat.

Outside on Leroux Street, a car with an Alabama license plate pulled up. A tired-looking couple got out and stretched. They must be the visitors their neighbors had told them they were expecting.

Even people from *Alabama* got to spend the Fourth of July in Flagstaff, Janey brooded.

She hated car trips.

"Look what I found," Janey's mother said, holding up a pair of fluorescent orange swim fins as she came into the garage. "I couldn't find the snorkel, though."

"Well, you can't really snorkel very well in Santa Monica Bay," her husband pointed out, running a hand back through his short black hair. "The waves are too high, and all you'd see is sand. We'll be able to use those flippers for body-surfing, though." He jammed them into the trunk.

"It'll be dark pretty soon," Janey's mother said,

peering outside the open garage door. "But we're not anywhere near ready to leave."

"We won't get out of here until nine o'clock at the earliest," Poppy said. "Not at the rate we're going."

"Then can I go over to Stacy's house to say good-bye?" Janey asked.

"You already said good-bye to your friends," her mother reminded her. "And we'll only be gone for a week, so don't bother making that face at me. But you *can* come inside and help me fold the laundry."

"Oh, thanks," Janey said, being as sarcastic as she dared.

Her father shot her a warning look, but his wife was off on another tangent. "Did you get the gas tank filled, Peter?" she was asking. "And those windshield wiper blades replaced?"

"It hasn't rained in months in Arizona *or* California," Poppy said, laughing. "But yeah—we have new wiper blades. And we're filled up to the brim, at about a million bucks a gallon. *Your mother*," he said to Janey, pretend-complaining.

Janey's mom gave a comic shrug. "I know I go a little overboard," she admitted. "I always say getting ready to leave is the worst part of any trip."

"Then why don't we just stay home?" Janey asked.

"We're staying *home*?" a shrill little voice squealed, and all heads turned to look at YoYo, who was standing at the doorway that led to the kitchen.

The little girl was wearing a long purple gauzy skirt with a droopy hem, part of an old Halloween costume, Janey suspected, an orange turtleneck sweater festooned with several strands of beads, and black patent leather party shoes. No socks. She was clutching Mousey, her favorite stuffed animal.

Mousey looked drab next to the glittering YoYo.

Norrie Bishop started to laugh. "Yolanda, what in the world do you have on?"

Five-year-old YoYo gave them a sunny grin. "My California clothes," she said, turning around so they could all admire her.

"Well, go change into your nightie," her mother told her firmly. "You know you're going to want to sleep in the car."

"I'm too excited to sleep," YoYo objected.

"Better do what Mommy says," Janey advised wearily. "Or else we'll *never* leave. And then we'll never get to come back home."

"I can't believe we're actually on our way," Janey's father said as the Bishops' car headed west out of town on Highway 40. They were going to drop down Route 89 through Prescott, he'd informed everyone, then drive down the mountain and cut on over to the interstate that would take them to California. It was the slow way, they admitted each year, but it was *their* way.

"And it's only ten-fifteen," her mother said, laughing as she checked her watch. "We're off like a herd of turtles."

"Where's Mousey?" YoYo screeched from the backseat. "Oh no, I left him at home!"

"Give us strength," Poppy groaned.

Her mother turned halfway around and tried to calm YoYo down. "I'm sure Mousey is somewhere in the car, honey. He's—"

"He's probably on top of my bed. Crying!" YoYo interrupted, frantic with worry.

"Do something, Peter," his wife pleaded.

"I'll turn the car around and we'll go back and get him," Poppy said, shaking his head. "It'll be easier than listening to *this* for the next hundred miles."

"Let's just keep going," Janey said. "She'll calm down after a while."

"I will not!" YoYo shouted.

"What possible difference could an extra twenty

minutes make?" Poppy asked reasonably. "I'm turning around."

"No, wait—here's Mousey," Janey's mother called out. "He was stuck under the front seat, that's all." She handed the floppy stuffed animal back to YoYo.

"Oh, Mousey," YoYo crooned. In the front seat, both parents sighed with relief.

"So, we're still on our way, apparently," Poppy said, adjusting his rearview mirror.

"Can we put our windows down now?" Janey asked. It was stuffy inside the car, but Poppy's allergies made him reluctant to use the air conditioner. He claimed it made things worse for him.

But really, Janey didn't mind; in fact, she preferred to have the windows down—especially on a long drive at night. The steady *whuh, whuh, whuh* of the tires on the road lulled her to sleep.

To sleep, to sleep, to sleep.

Janey opened her eyes. Her mother was stroking the back of Poppy's neck, and they were laughing. "Where are we?" Janey asked drowsily.

"Just south of Prescott," her father said. "The road will be pretty steep and curvy while we're heading down the mountain, but then it will straighten out.

And we'll be in California before you know it."

"Go on back to sleep, honey," her mother said, looking over her shoulder. "Get some rest. That way at least one of us will be able to face tomorrow with a smile."

"Maybe Janey doesn't feel like smiling," Peter Bishop reminded his wife playfully. "She's mad at us, remember? For dragging her with us on this trip?"

"I'm so not mad anymore," Janey told him. And she wasn't. It was as though her family was in their own private world, now, driving through the night.

"Oh, good," her mother said, reaching over the backseat to squeeze Janey's hand. "Now you can be our little snuggle-bunny again."

"Let's not get revolting about this," Janey said — although it was kind of nice being called snuggle-bunny once more. YoYo usually hogged all the cuddle words these days.

Not that Janey *needed* them, she told herself.

"Poppy's little snuggle-bunny," her father called back to her, joining the fun.

"The best kid in the world," Mommy said, nodding her head as if she'd just taken a vote, and Jane Elizabeth Bishop had won.

Janey laughed quietly and settled back into her

seat, preparing to fall back asleep. "I love you guys," she said, half under her breath.

But they'd heard. "We love you, too, Miss Jane," her mother told her. "That's for sure."

"And we always will, honey."

$\int$ally Warner is the author of many highly acclaimed novels for young people, including *Sort of Forever* and *How to Be a Real Person (In Just One Day)*. She and her husband live in Southern California with a miniature wirehaired dachshund, Rocky.

For more information about Ms. Warner and her books, visit her website: www.sallywarner.com.